I Smell Like Ham

I Smell Like Ham

Betty Hicks

Roaring Brook Press

Brookfield, Connecticut

Copyright © 2002 by Betty Hicks

Published by Roaring Brook Press
A division of The Millbrook Press, 2 Old New Milford Road
Brookfield, Connecticut 06804

Library of Congress Cataloging-in-Publication Data
Hicks, Betty.
I smell like ham/Betty Hicks.
p. cm.
Summary: Nick tries to maintain his sense of integrity as he works to suc-
ceed on the school basketball team, adjust to his new stepmother and "dorky"
stepbrother, and deal with peer pressure from his friends.
[1. Self-esteem—Fiction. 2. Conduct of life—Fiction. 3. Stepfamilies—Fic-
tion. 4. Basketball—Fiction. 5. Peer pressure—Fiction. 6. Schools—Fiction.]
I. Title.
PZ7.H53155 Is 2002
[Fic]—dc21   2002021951

Designed by Filomena Tuosto
Set in Bembo

First edition
ISBN 0-7613-1748-1(trade)
3 5 7 9 10 8 6 4 2

ISBN 0-7613-2857-2 (library binding)
3 5 7 9 10 8 6 4 2

Printed in the United States of America

For Bill and Nate and Lise,
who assumed,
from the very beginning,
that this would happen

The Wish

What did you learn in school today?" should win the Stupid-Question Award. Every time Dad asks me that, I want to wave a magic wand and zap myself into another family. Not because I never learn anything, but because I never learn the stuff Dad likes.

He craves genius—like knowing that earthquakes create seismic waves. Or that the number of atoms in a pound of iron is five trillion trillion.

Not every scientific fact rates, though. For example, don't say that the white part of bird droppings is pee—especially don't say it at the dinner table.

Yesterday I was practicing my dribbling when Dad pulled into the carport. The first thing he said when he stepped out of the car was "So, Nick, what did you learn in school today?"

"Well," I said, thumping the basketball extra hard into the pavement, "I learned that I'll never bring the ball downcourt without Carson Jones stealing it—not even if I practice every day."

I rested the ball on my hip.

"Not even if I practice every minute, Dad. You should see him. I might as well hand him the ball."

Dad scrunched his forehead up and looked mystified. His eyebrows actually twist when he does that —almost like he's wringing them out to dry. It's amazing. I've tried to make mine do that, but they just sit there.

"Oh . . . uh . . . I see," he said. "Well . . . keep practicing. You'll do fine."

I knew exactly what was coming next.

"Never say *never*."

Bingo! Good old Dad's well-meant, useless words of wisdom. He's got a million of them.

He leaned back into his car, pulled out a bunch of shirts on hangers, then turned to me. "Um, Nick, what I really meant was, what did you learn in math?"

Math? I couldn't even remember math. I remembered basketball. My first practice. It had started out great.

•   •   •

"Nick," Coach had called, reading my name off the roster. "You take the point guard spot."

Yes! I'd pumped my fist and leaped onto the floor. One of the best things about being in middle school —finally—was having a new coach. He had no way of knowing how lousy I'd been last year.

Josh inbounded the ball to me, and I did exactly what I'd practiced all summer. I took off, pumping the ball like a pro, focused, head up, eyes front. I even kept the ball low.

Whoosh. Carson came out of nowhere, stole the ball, then laid it up for two points. I looked to see if any of the guys were laughing at me. No, they were all staring at Carson like he was the next Michael Jordan.

The second and third time Carson stole it, I didn't bother to look. I stared at the floor while my cheeks burned, but I heard the laughter. The fourth time he did it, so much blood rushed to my ears, the roar drowned out the laughs.

I wanted to die. Instead, I smiled like a dork at Coach, but he was too busy scribbling on his note-pad to notice me, probably scratching out my name. Putting happy faces next to Carson's.

"Okay, Nick," said Coach. "Take a break. Paul, you sub for Nick."

I slumped onto the bench, blinking back a whole bunch of tears that were swimming around, making the gym floor blurry. When I could see again, I watched Paul. He didn't do any better than I had.

That made me feel better, but what difference did it make? Coach would be nuts not to start Carson at point guard.

"Nick," Dad repeated, draping the shirts over his shoulder. "Math. Did you learn anything new in math?"

"No," I answered. Why bother telling him what I'd really learned? That if I was going to practice at home, I'd need somebody better than Penelope to guard me.

Penelope is my neighbor's cat, and she'd rather pounce on a ball than roll in catnip. But she's a lousy substitute for Carson.

I followed Dad into the house, hauled myself up to my room, shut the door, and dove onto my bed. Sir Kay went flying.

"Scraggly old bear," I muttered, scooping him up off the floor. His fur had thinned so much I could see the fabric underneath, but his eyes were still black and shiny, like new.

I'm way too old to have a bear, but I put him back

on my pillow anyway, stretched out, and kicked off my sneakers.

"I *have* learned a lot," I declared out loud. As a matter of fact, the way my knowledge is piling up, I could be a genius before I turn twelve.

I stared at the grease spots on the ceiling where I'd lobbed chunks of Gloop. Add x's and o's, and they'd look just like a diagram of Coach's plays.

I punched the air. Yep. A genius.

Not for the stuff in textbooks. I mean real stuff. Like knowing too many Gummi Bears make you want to barf. And there's no warning. None. Number twenty-seven tastes great. Then number twenty-eight hits your stomach like a giant glueball. *Whump.*

Or knowing to be specific when I make wishes. I learned that a few months ago, when Dad hit me with the good news. *His* good news, that is.

"Nickel," he'd said, ruffling my hair.

He calls me Nickel when I make him happy, and Nicholas Knight Kimble when I don't.

"Nickel," he said, "you're finally going to get your wish."

Something about the way he said it—cheerful, but kind of nervous—got me worried. That and the fact that he's not the type who remembers wishes. Since

Mom died, he's never even remembered what I want for breakfast.

His eyebrows twisted. He ran his fingers up through his used-to-be-thick black hair. Then he loosened his tie, not once, but three times, as if he didn't know he'd already done it.

"What wish?" I asked.

"You know." His voice was soft and kind of sappy—the way it sounded when he called Mrs. Mitchell to ask her out.

"The wish that you had a brother," he said.

"Oh." The word popped out sounding exactly how I felt, sort of flat . . . and sinking.

It's true. I had spent my whole life wishing for a brother. But I'd imagined a three-day-old baby that Mom and Dad brought home from the hospital— one that Mom had given birth to.

She died two years ago. Dad clearly had some other baby in mind.

Then it hit me.

"Dwayne." I whispered the name like it was a disease, but I knew in my gut that Dwayne Mitchell, Dwayne-the-Dweeb Mitchell, was about to be my stepbrother.

The Promise 2

Dwayne Mitchell, my new stepbrother, is the nerdiest kid in the third grade, maybe even in the entire world. Two weeks ago, on Saturday, October 10, at 11:00 on a rainy morning, his mom married my dad.

I've learned a lot since then.

1. Weddings are overrated.
2. Too much wedding cake is almost as bad as too many Gummi Bears.
3. Dwayne's mother is a better cook than Dad.
4. My bedroom door won't lock.

When I first opened my eyes this morning, I'd almost forgotten that he lived here—until I focused on my bookshelf.

"Dwayne!"

King Arthur was missing. Right between *The High King* and *The Castle in the Attic*, a big, fat, empty space shouted at me.

Mom and Dad gave me my first book about knights before I was born—because they'd picked Knight to be my middle name. After that, they added to my collection because I ended up loving all that stuff about chivalry and honor, especially King Arthur and his Knights of the Round Table.

I barely heard the puny knock at my door.

"It's not locked," I grumbled. Because it won't lock.

As the door inched open, Dwayne stuck his head through. Then he slipped inside. Dwayne's pretty small to begin with, but next to my life-size Michael Jordan poster he looked like a mouse.

He stood frozen in front of my wadded-up sweatshirt and socks. I'm guessing he'd never seen clothes on the floor before.

"Where's *King Arthur?*" I asked, pointing to the bookshelf.

"I borrowed it," he squeaked.

Geez, I thought. He even sounds like a mouse.

I wanted to pull the sheets over my head and wish myself back to the Dark Ages, or the Middle Ages, or whenever it was that knighthood was everywhere. Instead I propped myself up on my elbow and said, "Ever heard of privacy?"

"I'm sorry," he answered, his voice all quivery. "I wanted to draw some of the pictures."

His head drooped, but his slicked-down red hair didn't move. My hair flops around like a horse's mane. Dwayne's could have been carved in wood.

He stared down at his clean white sneakers—not a scuff on them. Dark pants with the crease ironed in. A t-shirt that was tucked in neater than an army cot.

He looked up and smiled. "Don't you like the one where Arthur is pulling the sword out—"

"Next time, ask, okay?"

"Okay," he whispered, backing out the door.

Man, what did I do to deserve this?

He draws. He reads. Doesn't he ever go outside? He can't throw. He can't catch. I bet he thinks dunking is something you do with a doughnut.

I hated to sound so mean, but honestly, I couldn't help it. Too much time with Dwayne would put the Pope in a bad mood.

"L.B.D." I had scrawled it all over my notebook, in the columns of my homework, inside my desk drawer. "Life Before Dwayne." Just me and Dad. It had been so easy.

Now there was somebody who actually liked

telling Dad what he learned in school. Who snooped around my room. Who could embarrass me in front of my friends just by being there.

And why did his mom let him dress like a nerd? And act like a baby? Where the heck was his dad, anyway?

And why did I care? Didn't I have bigger problems? Hadn't I just played my best at practice and I still stunk?

I reached down and lifted Sir Kay off the floor, where he'd fallen during the night. Out of the corner of my eye, I spotted Mom's picture smiling at me from my bedside table.

It was the same smile she'd always had when she used to call me her superstar.

"*Sir* Superstar," I would grin and correct her.

"Ah, yes," she'd say. "Nick, my noble knight. *Sir* Superstar."

I placed Sir Kay against my pillow, then slipped back under the covers and curled up. I squeezed my eyes shut so I couldn't see the photograph.

Why was I worrying about Dwayne? I needed to worry about how stupid *I* was. So stupid I promised my mother—at her funeral, for Pete's sake—that I'd be a real superstar. A basketball superstar. Just for her. Every day her picture reminded me.

Magic 3

I thought about asking Dad for help. He's not one of those dads who falls all over himself helping his kid with sports, but he'll practice with me if I really need it.

Doing things with Dad has gotten tricky, though. Miriam is here.

Miriam. That's what I call Mrs. Mitchell now that she's my stepmother. She isn't so bad, except when she says things like, "Nick, your floor seems to be missing. Do you remember the last time anyone saw it?"

The problem is, I never get Dad to myself anymore, not even for a second. She's everywhere. Her and Duh-wayne.

So I decided to practice at Magic's house. I named him that when we were in kindergarten. Not after the basketball player, but because he could disappear like magic whenever we got in trouble. Everyone's called him that ever since. Even his mother.

On my way through the kitchen, I grabbed a banana off the counter. Dwayne stood on a footstool, cracking eggs into a mixing bowl.

Geez. A miniature chef. I bet he reads cookbooks.

When I got to Magic's, he was washing his dad's car in the driveway.

"What's up?"

"Mount Everest," he answered.

I smiled. "Want to shoot some hoops?"

"Sure," he said. "Soon as I finish this."

He had his dad's Jeep so lathered up that it looked like a bubble bath. I scooped up a handful of suds and threw it in his hair.

Mistake. Magic is so skinny he could walk through prison bars, but he's a lot taller than me. And he had the garden hose.

The next thing I knew, I was wetter than soup.

So I tackled him.

He squirted water up my shirt.

I wrestled the nozzle out of his hand and shot water down his pants.

"Nicholas Kimble!" Magic's mother sounded a lot like Dad.

I dropped the hose. It landed on the squeeze-part of the handle and squirted me in the face.

"What do you think you're doing? And where's Magic? He's supposed to be washing the car."

Magic? Wasn't he here? I wiped my face and looked around, but he'd vanished. It was a talent.

"Never mind." She shook her head. "He'll turn up. Come inside and borrow some dry clothes."

Some October days are as warm as summer, but today wasn't one of them. The wind cut through my soppy sweatshirt like flying icicles.

When I got to Magic's room, he was already there, wearing dry clothes and looking so innocent you'd have thought he'd just helped four old ladies cross the interstate.

I pulled on a pair of his jeans, then rolled each leg up about a mile. He tossed me a t-shirt.

I sniffed it.

"It's clean." Magic held up his right hand. "I swear."

It smelled like the inside of a fish tank to me, but I put it on anyway, then threw a ratty flannel shirt over it.

Down the hall, I heard Magic's parents arguing.

"Move it," said Magic, pulling me out the door and shoving me down the stairs.

We went back outside and rinsed the car. The soap had dried, so it took forever. Then Magic remembered his basketball was flat, and he couldn't find the pump.

"We can practice at your house," he said.

Inside, I groaned. For weeks I'd been making up reasons not to bring friends to my house. I hated them seeing what a dork Dwayne was. Still, I had to face facts. Small as he was, he was too big to hide until I went to college.

"Yeah, okay," I muttered. Besides, Magic was the least likely of my friends to notice whether somebody was a loser or not.

As we headed toward home, I had a great thought. Maybe Magic could teach Duh-wayne to disappear.

Motor Mouth 4

Magic bombed through my back door and into the kitchen five steps ahead of me. He always made himself at home, like this was his house, not mine. I hoped Miriam wasn't too big on manners.

"Hi," I heard him say. "You must be Dwayne. What's up?"

Dwayne. Why wasn't he in his room reading the encyclopedia? No, he stood at the kitchen counter wearing an apron. An *apron*! Flour streaked his face while he smoothed chocolate icing on a pound cake like he was getting a grade on it.

"Cake!" exclaimed Magic.

"Have a piece," said Dwayne, sounding so proud you'd have thought he'd invented sugar.

"Thanks," said Magic, reaching for a plate while

Dwayne cut the cake. "Maybe you could show my little brother how to do something useful."

Magic could find something nice to say to anybody.

The kitchen smelled all warm and chocolaty. Maybe having a brother who made cakes was a good thing. Except for the apron.

Dwayne beamed and slid a piece of cake onto the plate.

Magic pulled out a chair and plopped himself down at the kitchen table. "*Grtmp. Stmph,*" he mumbled, shoveling globs of chocolate into his mouth. It didn't take much to make Magic happy.

"Want a piece?" Dwayne asked.

"Sure," I answered, wondering how it tasted. Magic was no test. He'd eat anything. I took a bite. It was good. Now even Dwayne was a better cook than my dad.

"I didn't know you could cook *good* stuff," I said.

Dwayne giggled. "Next time, ask," he said. Little lights danced in his eyes while he tried to stifle a goofy grin.

I couldn't believe it. Duh-wayne was making fun of me. I looked to see if Magic had noticed. Nope. He was licking icing off his fingers.

I shot Dwayne a look that said, "You-are-so-*not-*

funny." Then I ate the cake. No point wasting perfectly good cake.

"Hello, boys."

Miriam. Looking majorly energetic and healthy
in her blue warm-ups. I ate faster.

"Hi, Mrs. Kimble," said Magic.

I'd never get used to the fact that *she* was Mrs.
Kimble now.

"I'm Magic."

Miriam hesitated.

"That's his name," I muttered.

"Oh." She laughed and slipped into the chair next
to him. "Nice to meet you, Magic. What are you
boys up to?"

Magic wiped his mouth on his sleeve.

I watched Miriam to see if she flinched. No, but
she did pass him a napkin.

I hoped he wouldn't lick his plate.

"We're headed outside to shoot some hoops,"
Magic answered.

"Right," I said, standing up and shoving my chair
back.

"If Nick and I don't practice," Magic added,
"we're gonna be warming the bench again this
year."

I fired off a look that said, "Stop talking. Now."

I didn't want Miriam and Duh-wayne to know what went on at practice, or school, or anywhere. Besides, Magic would not be warming the bench. He had locks on being center because he'd grown six inches since last year. All he had to do was stand under the basket and he'd be better than anybody.

"I'm working on my hook shot"— Magic's mouth kept running— "and Nick's dribbling like a pro, only. . ." He stopped.

"Only what?" asked Miriam.

"Nothing." Magic looked apologetically at me.

Miriam waited.

"Well, nothing much," he said. "Nick just had kind of a bad practice."

This couldn't be happening.

"Oh?" said Miriam, looking at me expectantly.

"It wasn't so bad," I mumbled.

"Yeah," Magic jumped back in. "It wasn't even Nick's fault."

I sat back down so I could kick him under the table.

"I mean, Carson stole the ball a lot." Magic kept yakking as if I hadn't just scraped the flesh right off his shin. "Not because Nick's no good. It's because Carson's so awesome."

Maybe he was trying to make me look good, but

in two minutes, Magic had handed Miriam more information than I'd given her in two weeks.

She stared at me. Concern dripped off her face. *Her* eyebrows did not twist. They curved up and down, gracefully, oozing pity.

"Yeah, well, we're out of here." I stood up again. "Thanks for the cake, Dwayne." Even I knew this was not a good time to call him Duh-wayne.

Miriam gathered up her dark, shiny hair and twisted a rubber band around it. "Let's all play," she suggested in a sunshiny voice that sparkled all over the kitchen.

"Great," said Magic.

My eyes burned deep into Magic's brain, asking, "Are you crazy?" But he was too busy licking his plate to notice.

One Slam, No Dunks 5

I dragged myself upstairs and changed into my own clothes. I was in no hurry to play ball with Miriam and Dwayne.

I know I'm not supposed to care what friends think, but so far I'm not too good at it. Dwayne is embarrassing, with or without the apron.

There's also the promise I made to Mom, which was dumb, but I meant to keep it, so I needed to practice. Hard. Now. Not waste time with family basketball-bonding.

I've also learned how grown-ups think, and I knew that by the end of next week Coach would have me tagged—good or bad—forever.

Outside, Magic, Miriam, and Dwayne waited under the basket Dad had put up for me, regulation height, ten feet. I'd had to nag him for months, but when Dad finally gets around to doing something, he does it right.

When I showed up, Dwayne looked nervous. Miriam looked cheerful. Magic looked relieved. I looked at all three of them and wished I were in my room, reading about Lancelot galloping around, wasting a bunch of dragons.

Miriam held my basketball on one hip and rubbed her chin with the other hand. I had a terrible feeling she was trying to remember what piece of equipment was missing—like a bat or a hockey stick.

Duh-wayne shifted back and forth from one foot to the other, studying his too-white shoelaces. Maybe we did have something in common. Neither of us wanted to play basketball with his mother.

Magic must have decided to make the most of it, because he started shooting imaginary jump shots and grinning as if he were running for Mister Nice Guy.

"So," said Miriam. "What'll it be? Ball-handling drills, one-on-one, or would you boys rather just sit around and watch me slam dunk?"

Magic stopped his jump shot in midair and threw

a dropped-jaw look of surprise over his left shoulder. His hang time was spectacular. Then his feet hit the concrete with a thud.

My reaction was weirder. First I thought, Wow, maybe she's good. Then I got an achy knot in my chest, remembering Mom playing Horse with me. Having that same kind of fun with Miriam, especially if she was awesome, didn't seem right.

"Mrs. Kimble," said Magic, "can you really dunk?"

She laughed. "Not on my best day." She poked Magic in the arm. "But I got your attention."

They both laughed like hyenas. Then Miriam dished him the ball and he went in for a lay-up.

Dwayne stopped staring at his feet and giggled. I even chuckled, relieved she wasn't Supermom, but also thinking this might actually go better than I'd feared.

It didn't.

We voted to play Miriam and me versus Dwayne and Magic. Magic inbounded the ball to Dwayne, who dropped it, then kicked it out of bounds while he was trying to pick it back up. It rolled down the embankment and disappeared into our neighbor's hedge, with Penelope stalking it.

"My fault," Magic apologized as he scrambled down the bank. "I threw it too hard!" he shouted back. He and Penelope both vanished into the bushes.

Dwayne went back to staring at his feet.

I clenched my teeth and pretended to be calm.

When Magic reappeared with the ball, his arms were covered with scratches but he was smiling.

I wasn't.

As much as I hated being stuck with Dwayne, I hated Magic being stuck with him even more.

I took a deep breath and inbounded the ball to Miriam, who dribbled toward the basket with Magic guarding her. She dribbled way too high. Magic could easily have stolen the ball. But he didn't. Instead he blocked the lane.

Miriam dribbled with her back to Magic, then pivoted and arced this perfect hook shot over his head. Well, it would have been perfect, if she'd released the ball later. Instead, it soared over the basket and lodged between the garage roof and the back of the backboard.

My face flushed so hot I expected to see smoke oozing from my ears.

For the next fifteen minutes, Magic and I got the ladder down from the hooks in the garage and retrieved the ball. We didn't say much.

"I'm sorry," Miriam apologized.

"Hey, not to worry," said Magic, grinning again. "Your form was great!"

Didn't he ever get mad?

Dwayne sat cross-legged on the grass stroking Penelope, who had draped herself over his legs as if she'd melted. Even that bugged me. I could never catch Penelope, much less pet her. The cat was hyper. If Dad weren't so allergic, I'd have a dog.

Dwayne placed Penelope lovingly on the grass and edged timidly back to the driveway. Magic threw him the ball. Well, handed him the ball is a better description.

I trapped him against the end line. He wrapped his arms around the ball, hugging it to his chest and making a T sign with his hands.

"Time out!" he screamed.

"Geez!" I shouted. "We're never gonna play. I've been out here thirty minutes, and I haven't even dribbled the ball. I need to practice . . . *practice!* Not baby-sit a dorky little wimp."

Dwayne loosened his grip on the ball and slowly unfolded his arms. His head lowered as he gazed sadly down at the ball, as if it were a puppy I'd just crushed with a hammer. The ball rolled off his limp arms and bounced noisily down the driveway. Penelope bounded after it.

I could see Dwayne's chin quivering, even with his head down. He bolted into the house.

Miriam glared at me, her teeth clenched and her hands balled up so tight I could see blue veins.

Oh, no, I thought, what have I done?

She spun around and followed Dwayne.

Right at that instant, I learned something colossally important about moms. They're like bears . . . and you never, ever mess with their cubs. If I had a real mother, I might have known that.

Still, I felt about two inches tall. Why had I called him a dork and a wimp? Well, to be honest, he was a dork and a wimp—*and* a baby.

But if I'd known then what I found out later, I never would have said it.

I turned toward Magic, but he had already vanished.

No More Frosted Flakes 6

Nicholas! Come to dinner," Dad called.

Not Nick. Not Nickel. Not even Nicholas Knight Kimble, which would have meant Dad was angry. "Nicholas" stood for something worse. It told me I had let Dad down.

I ran a bunch of excuses for skipping dinner through my head. Not hungry, too much homework, room needs cleaning, gangsters holding me at gunpoint, hoof-and-mouth disease.

None rang true.

I dragged myself to dinner. I knew Miriam had told Dad that I'd made Dwayne cry. I'd heard their worried-parent voices in the kitchen.

The atmosphere when I sat down at the table reminded me of Mom's funeral. Heavy. Awkward.

Everybody wanting to make things happier, but nobody knowing the right thing to say.

Miriam sat so straight her back didn't come close to touching the chair. Dad leaned back, took a deep breath, and sighed. Dwayne fidgeted in his seat. I stared down at my food.

Yow! What was this garbage on my plate?

I cut my eyes at Dad, whose return gaze said, "Watch it, son, you're already on thin ice."

"This looks great," I said, smiling feebly at Miriam. "Uh, what is it?"

"Scrambled tofu," she answered politely, without looking at me, "with wild mushrooms, peppers, and curry."

"Oh," I said, hoping I sounded enthusiastic.

For two weeks, Miriam had been cooking all my favorite food. Hamburgers, barbecued chicken, macaroni and cheese. She'd even made homemade pizza. But the last couple of meals had gotten weird.

Something she claimed was lasagna had spinach and squash where the good stuff should have been. Then we had a giant fungus on a bun that she said was a *porta-something* mushroom burger. *Porta-potty* stuck in my mind, but that wasn't it.

Now there was a pile of yellow chunks on my

plate that looked like someone had thrown up on them.

"What a mess," said Dad. "Just when I thought the layout for the new entertainment section was ready, we ran into a snag."

Huh? He wasn't talking about tofu. He was talking about work. Did that mean he wasn't mad at me? Or just not ready to yell at me in front of Miriam yet?

"Can I help?" asked Miriam.

She freelances for the paper. Dad's the editor. That's how they met. They talk about newspaper stuff all the time. After dinner they play Scrabble.

When Mom was alive, Dad never talked about work. We talked about school, sports, that kind of stuff. After dinner we all watched *Jeopardy*.

I glanced from Dad to Miriam, then back to Dad. They gabbed away about work—some article Miriam was writing. Dwayne nibbled his food with his head down. All I could see was his perfectly parted hair.

Everything's so different.

Food, time with Dad, rules, privacy, you name it. Even the house has changed. Fluffy, flowery pillows on the sofa. An art book on the coffee table where Dad used to stack the mail. Wheat bran instead of frosted flakes. A bathroom that smells like flower petals.

And Dwayne.

I jabbed my fork into a chunk of tofu and took a bite. Spicy lumps of barf. Good flavor, gross feel.

It's not that I was glad I'd hurt his feelings. In fact, I felt awful. Like a rottweiler who'd attacked a toy poodle.

And definitely not like a knight. Whoever heard of Lancelot charging around, blowing out helpless vassals?

"Nicholas," said Dad. His voice had a flat, hollow sound—disappointment. "Answer me, son."

I looked up. They were staring at me. Miriam and Dad. Not Dwayne. He'd stopped nibbling, though.

Were they talking about me yelling at Dwayne? Parents do that. They bring up the bad stuff just when you've dropped your guard.

"Well?" asked Dad, putting his fork down.

"What?" I answered.

"What do you have to say for yourself?"

That was another question I hated. I had nothing to say for myself. But *nothing* was a bad answer.

"Nick didn't do anything," said Dwayne, his voice so small he could have been at the bottom of a well. "I'm just no good at sports."

"Oh, honey," said Miriam. "You did fine. I'm the one who needs lessons."

She smiled at Dwayne.

It was my turn now—to be honorable. I knew it. I swallowed. "You both did fine," I lied, mashing my fork into my tofu.

"Dwayne," I said, "I'm sorry I called you those names." I looked right at him and said it like I meant it, because I did mean it. I *was* sorry.

I still didn't want to play ball with him, though, but I didn't say that.

"It's okay," he answered.

The room stayed real quiet for a while. Dwayne took a bite of mushroom. Miriam relaxed into her chair a little. Dad picked his fork back up.

"So," Miriam said finally, "let's talk about you. And how you can make the team."

I didn't want to talk about that, but I could tell Miriam was trying not to hate me.

"In sixth grade," I explained, "everybody makes the team. It's a rule. But unless you're one of the starters, you're lucky to play for more than half a second."

"Well," said Miriam, "Michael Jordan didn't even make the team his sophomore year in high school."

"How'd you know that?" I asked.

"Miriam was in college with Michael. At UNC," said Dad.

"I played in the pep band," she announced proudly. "So I got to go to every home game. I watched Michael Jordan, Sam Perkins, James Worthy—"

"No kidding?" I was amazed. "That's really cool. What were they like? Was Jordan's number 23 then, too? Can you call him up on the phone?"

"They were great," she said. "You know, nice. And Michael's number *was* 23, but no, I can't call him up. I doubt he'd—"

"Do you have his autograph? Did you ever play ball with him? I mean a pickup game or something?"

"Nick," said Dad, trying to sound strict, "slow down and let her answer." But he was glad we were talking. I could tell.

"No autograph," said Miriam. "And no pickup game. I'm a fan, not a player. As you already know," she added.

I blushed and looked down.

"I know from watching what a player *should* do. I just can't do it. And Nick," she reached over and gently touched my arm, "I'd love to help you if I can."

"Thanks," I said, but that achy knot in the middle

of my chest came back, as though Mom might be watching.

Then Dwayne chimed in. "You could be another Bob Pettit."

"Who?" I never heard of Bob Pettit.

"The NBA's most valuable player in 1956 and 1959," he answered.

1956 and 1959!? Dwayne wasn't born yet. Even Dad wasn't born yet. Where did he get this stuff?

Dwayne sat up straighter in his chair and started bouncing. His squeaky voice grew louder. "They cut him from his high school team twice. But he worked hours and hours in his backyard—just like you. And he ended up great!"

Dwayne's eyes sparkled. You'd think I had made the NBA. I knew they meant well, but this was crazy. I had a stepmother who learned basketball by watching, and a stepbrother who learned it by reading. What ever happened to playing?

My worries came crashing back. I had practice on Monday and I needed to *play* good. Not watch. Not read. If I expected to keep my promise to Mom, I needed to wipe Carson right off the court.

Ham Hair and Pickle Slime 7

The next day, Sunday, Dad and Miriam left the house early and drove two and a half hours to the Blue Ridge Parkway, just to see some colored leaves.

"Let's all go," Miriam had suggested.

No, thanks. I hadn't forgotten the results of "Let's all play." Besides, leaf viewing sounded about as exciting to me as a nap.

"Sounds great," I said, "but I need to practice."

"And I need to write a science report," said Dwayne.

Which made me the baby-sitter. "Dad," I complained.

"I won't be any trouble," Dwayne insisted.

And, believe it or not, he wasn't. He didn't spend much time on his science report, either. Mostly he sat on the side of the driveway and watched Magic and me. Penelope snuggled in his lap while he practically stroked her bald.

She was so happy with Dwayne she never pounced once.

He didn't ask to play. I didn't offer.

My apology at dinner had smoothed things out on the surface, but underneath, an edgy feeling lurked. Dwayne and Miriam tiptoed around me as if I were armed and dangerous.

I drew a big square with chalk, ten feet by ten feet. I dribbled the ball inside the boundaries, with Magic inside guarding me, trying to steal it. Coach said that was a great way to learn to use your body to shield the ball.

We dribbled from noon until dark. I had calluses on my fingers. But I was ready for Carson.

Monday, I hopped out of bed without punching my snooze alarm. I even beat Dwayne to the bathroom. As I sudsed up my hair in the shower, I grinned. What would Dwayne do if I stayed in here so long he didn't have time to carve every hair into place?

Then I smelled food. Why did the bathroom smell like baked ham? I sniffed again. The odor seemed to be coming from the shampoo.

I couldn't believe it. My hair smelled like a TV dinner. It still reeked after I'd dried off and dressed.

"Miriam," I said, when I came downstairs to breakfast," how come the shampoo smells like ham?" My tone clearly implied that ham-scented shampoo was not normal.

"Ham?" said Miriam. She wrinkled her eyebrows together. "Oh, ham!" she exclaimed, then crumpled into a fit of laughter.

I jabbed a fork into the stack of pancakes on the counter, slapped four or five on my plate, and sat down.

Dad lowered his newspaper. Dwayne trotted in, stopped, and stared at his mother. She was still laughing.

"Oh, Nick," she said, wiping away tears with her fingertips. "It's not ham, it's cloves."

Cloves, I thought. What are cloves? Then I remembered. They're those tiny little brown knots with the stems that Mom used to stick all over ham before she baked it.

Why would anyone put them in shampoo?

"Miriam," asked Dad, "why would anyone put cloves in shampoo?"

Thank you, Dad.

Even Dwayne looked embarrassed.

"Organic products are nature's purest cleansers." She sounded like a commercial. "And Nick," she added, "cloves have tones that will make your brown hair richer."

Dad grunted and went back to his paper.

Dwayne speared two pancakes, sat down, and said, "Pass the syrup, please."

Did they think she had just given us a normal answer? Dad's hair was black. Was he going to shampoo with licorice? Would Dwayne get tomatoes?

I ate my pancakes in silence, thankful she hadn't put artichokes in them.

When I grabbed my backpack, I remembered I hadn't made my lunch. Mom used to fix it, but Dad said that was my job now.

Miriam would have done it—making healthy stuff that I could have traded with some girl for fat meaty sandwiches with cheese, but Dwayne ruined that deal when he found out I made my own lunch. He went nuts.

"Mom," he'd begged, "can I make mine, too? Pleeeeease."

As if fixing your lunch was a good thing. And Miriam agreed.

So now Dwayne's head was two feet into the refrigerator, checking out cream cheese and cucumbers, bread with giant seeds in it, sprouts, and more mushrooms I'd never heard of.

My bus came earlier than Dwayne's. I grabbed two pieces of bread and three slices of bologna, shoved them in a Baggie, and threw it all in my book bag.

As I dashed for the bus, I muttered ugly thoughts about my weird family. Then I pushed the delete key in my brain and clicked on basketball. My new moves. I couldn't wait.

But I did wait. And wait . . . and wait. By 11:30, I'd had assembly, English, math, and social studies.

I'd listened to a lecture about the importance of good citizenship. I'd learned that "varying sentence structure improves composition." I spent one whole period trying to figure out how to add and subtract decimals. I got a C on a map-skills test. And it wasn't even lunch yet.

At least we got to change classes. That was the good part about middle school. The bad part was pushing my way through the seventh and eighth graders who owned the halls. The trick was acting cool and humble at the same time.

Lunch—finally. Halfway to basketball practice! I slid into a seat across from Magic at a corner table. Sixth graders always sat in the corners.

"What're you going to be on Halloween?" asked Magic.

"Who knows?" I said. "King Arthur maybe. Or Lancelot."

"Great!" said Magic. "I'll be Merlin."

"Perfect."

"Hey, guys," said Carson, plopping down beside me. He unfolded his sandwich bag and pulled out a pickle and chips.

"What's up?" he asked.

"My social studies grade," said Magic, jabbing the air with a thumbs-up.

"No kidding?" I answered. "I got a crummy C."

"Ooooooooo," said Carson, imitating a spooky sound. "My crystal ball shows study hall in your future."

"Yeah, maybe." I shrugged. Meanwhile, I was thinking, my crystal ball shows that you won't steal the ball from me today, you jerk.

It's not that I don't like Carson. I like him fine. To tell the truth, I wouldn't mind *being* Carson. He's not only good at basketball, he's good at everything—even girls.

Me, I'm not all that goofy about girls. But lately I've been thinking I ought to at least learn how to talk to one. Especially Ali.

Then I saw her...Ali, I mean. Walking toward our table. She has great hair. Blond and silky. Even better, she knows the difference between a full-court press and getting back on defense.

"Hey, Ali." Carson casually motioned her over with the hand that held the pickle, then calmly took a bite. If I'd tried that I probably would have flung pickle slime all over her.

Magic slid over, and she sat down. Across from me. *Wham!* The door between my brain and my mouth slammed shut. Nick, I thought, get over this. She's just a girl.

I slid the bread and bologna out of my book bag. Smushed. Majorly, totally smushed.

"Uh, pass the mustard," I muttered while I fumbled with the bread slices, hoping I could will them into fluffing back out a little.

I shook the plastic mustard dispenser down hard over the mangled bread. Not hard enough. When I squeezed, air and mustard spit out so loud and gross that people three tables over laughed.

Carson turned sideways and sniffed. "Hey, did you know your hair smells like ham?"

While Ali and Magic leaned over the table to smell my hair, I prayed—please let basketball practice go better than this.

Grinch Drills 8

Coach stood in front of us, checking names off on his clipboard. Then he went over the rules. Another lecture. Wasn't it enough that I'd survived a whole day of classes? All I wanted to do was play ball.

"Rule number one," he said, holding one finger up. "Anyone late for practice runs extra suicide sprints."

Suicide sprints? What were they?

"Rule number two, anyone . . . " He paused to shake his clipboard at us. The pencil that was tied to the top dangled and bounced all over the place. "And I mean *anyone* who misses practice without an excuse won't play in the next game."

"A written excuse?" Carson interrupted.

"Verbal is fine," said Coach. "We have an honor code. I expect you to follow it."

"Coach," Magic asked, "what absences are excused?"

Coach's mouth turned up in a sneaky grin. His eyes twinkled with malice. He looked exactly like the Grinch Who Stole Christmas. He even had a pear-shaped head and a skinny neck.

"Death," he answered with an evil grin, "serious illness, and alien abduction."

Magic laughed, but no one else did. The only other sound was the squeak of bleacher seats, where the rest of us squirmed. Was he serious?

"Rule number three. No smoking."

Hey. Sometimes Carson smoked. I could turn him in and get rid of the competition. Starting point guard, here I come.

I sighed, knowing I'd never do that.

"Number four. I expect cooperation, good sportsmanship, and team play. No showoffs."

So far, so good, I thought. Just like being a knight. Dependable, committed, honest, fit, fair. If only I could dribble.

"Rule number five—"

Geez, I thought, when are we going to play?

"I want us to win, but even more important, I want us to have fun. Any questions?"

No! Let's play!

Silence, except for the bleacher seats, which were really squeaking now.

"Great," said Coach. "We scrimmaged at our first practice. That was to see what you could do. Today we're doing drills." He grinned the Grinch smile again. "Lots of drills."

I groaned. Everybody groaned.

We started with stretches. Then we did twenty push-ups. I thought my last three might be throw-ups.

Next we ran laps. Followed by a water break.

Everyone crowded around the water cooler gasping for breath.

"Is he for real?" Josh whispered. "He's gonna kill us."

"No kidding," said Magic, between slurps of water.

"Anybody besides me notice he looks like the Grinch?" I asked.

"You're right!" Carson exclaimed, choking on his water. "He really does."

He exploded into a brief coughing fit, then wiped his mouth with the back of his hand. "Do you think he's kidding about the excuses?" he wheezed. "I mean, come on. Death and alien abduction?"

"You could die and we'd find out." I gave him a push.

"Right," said Carson, shoving me back, "or your little brother could abduct me. I hear he's an alien."

Everybody laughed.

"Yeah," I said, laughing the loudest. "He'd probably dissect your brain and study it. Too bad he wouldn't find anything."

Coach blew the whistle. "This is a water break, boys, not a tea party."

Saved by the whistle. But now I knew the word was out—my stepbrother was one big joke.

For the next thirty minutes, we did speed drills, agility drills, jumping drills.

I tried not to think about Dwayne. I tried not to think about the fact that we weren't even going to play today. Mostly I thought about trying to breathe.

"C-c-coach," Paul stammered, panting like a dog, "when do we get to touch the ball?"

"Ball?" said Coach. "Oh, yeah." He chuckled.

We sucked down more water, then shot foul shots. Coach explained that it's good to practice free throws when you're tired, because it's harder. No kidding. I made one out of five.

Just when I could breathe again, Coach declared he had an idea.

"Yeah," Carson moaned, "the Grinch got a wonderful, awful idea."

That cracked everybody up.

"Ah," said Coach. "You boys think suicide sprints are funny. All right then . . . enjoy."

We started on the end line, sprinted to the top of the key, touched the floor, then sprinted back. Without stopping we touched the floor and sprinted again—this time to the half-court line—touched, then back to where we started.

"You're halfway there," shouted Coach.

Halfway? Did he say halfway? I hoped I looked good on a stretcher.

We touched the floor, and kept running—this time to the top of the key at the other end of the court. Touch. Sprint all the way back to the beginning. Floor touch. Then a full-court sprint and back again.

While my chest heaved, my lungs sucked air like two tornadoes. My thighs burned out of control. And my feet didn't even belong to me.

Coach blew his whistle. "Good work, boys. As a reward, we'll scrimmage for the last fifteen minutes."

Scrimmage! I could hardly stand.

We took another water break, but nobody said a word. We were all too busy breathing and standing.

Coach divided us into two teams. Carson played point guard for the green team. I played point for the gold.

Josh inbounded the ball to me. I slogged my way downcourt, way too tired to run, but I did shield the ball with my body, just like I'd practiced. Carson shuffled along beside me. He didn't even try to steal it.

Was I that good, or was he that tired? Who cared? I got it downcourt!

I pulled up at the top of the key and spotted Magic moving toward the basket. Looking straight at him, I fired a bounce pass down the lane.

Carson swooped in and picked it off smoother than King Arthur's falcon snatching up a field mouse. Then he turned and dribbled straight back downcourt for an easy lay-up.

I watched, frozen.

Coach jotted something in his notes.

I huffed quick, short breaths through my nose and blinked a lot to keep from crying.

Mentally, I started a new list of what I'd learned.

1. Don't telegraph my passes.

Clouds 9

What did you learn in school today?" Dad asked.

I sat at the dinner table, starving but too tired to lift my fork.

I learned to put mustard on my sandwich before leaving the house, I thought. I learned not to wash my hair with cloves, not to telegraph my passes, and never to be late for basketball practice because a single extra suicide sprint would kill me.

I also learned that most of the sixth grade knows Dwayne's a dork, and that I will never be better than Carson Jones.

"I learned how to subtract decimals," I mumbled.

"Good," Dad nodded, lifting a forkful of sesame noodles to his mouth. "That's very good. Anything else?"

"Nope," I answered.

"How about basketball practice?"

"Fine," I said.

"Fine? How fine?" he asked. "Did the NBA make you an offer?"

"Not exactly," I answered. Sometimes Dad could be kind of funny. But I wasn't in the mood. The whole basketball thing was too depressing. And we were having weird food again.

"You're a real fountain of information," said Dad, shaking his head. "Dwayne, how about your day?"

"Mrs. Bissel liked my science report," he declared.

"You researched clouds, right?"

"The Oort cloud," Dwayne answered.

The Oort cloud. What the heck was an Oort cloud? I wondered. Every kid in the third grade learned about rain and cumulus clouds, but good old Duh-wayne was reading up on Oort clouds.

"What's the Oort cloud?" asked Dad, so interested that he stopped chewing.

Miriam smiled proudly.

"It's a collection of big dirty snowballs that circle the solar system way outside the orbit of Pluto. Sometimes they become comets and . . . "

Oh, gag, I thought. Dad is going to eat up every brainy word of this.

Carefully, I picked the green things out of my

noodles. Oort clouds, I thought. Big dirty snowballs in space. It reminded me of black ice. That's what Mom's car skidded on when she had her wreck—rain that freezes on the road and looks like harmless water, only it's not harmless at all.

In the hospital, the day before she died, she'd squeezed my hand and called me her superstar.

I tried to grin and say "*Sir* Superstar," like I always did, but the words jammed in the back of my throat, trapped there by the ache.

She had waited, her smile turning sad when she realized I couldn't say the words.

So later, at her funeral, I decided to promise her I really would be a star, a basketball star—for her.

Now I wish I'd never whispered it. What happens if you break a promise to your dead mother? It's too terrible to think about.

Maybe she wouldn't mind if I were a star at something else. Not school or sports. What was left? It was five hundred years too late for knighthood.

I twirled a ball of noodles on my plate. Think about something else.

Knights. At least I could be what I wanted for one night. Halloween. Five nights away, and I had my costume figured out, almost.

I'd molded a shield out of an old foil roasting pan, and I had a plastic sword that looked pretty real. If I could get my hands on another roasting pan, I'd make an armored breastplate and be Lancelot. If not, I'd grab an aluminum pie pan from the kitchen, carve it into a crown, and go as King Arthur.

Maybe Magic's mom had an extra roasting pan. Or maybe—

"How about it, Nick?" asked Dad.

"How about what?" I answered. Had he finished admiring Oorts already?

"Halloween," he said.

"Right." I nodded. "I'm going to be a knight."

"Good. Dwayne'll like that, won't you, buddy?"

Dwayne? Oh, no. What had I missed? I looked at Dwayne. He was eyeing me the way a kid with no money eyes the clerk in a candy store.

Miriam seemed nervous.

"Nick won't mind," Dad assured her.

"Mind what?" I asked.

"Taking Dwayne with you on Halloween," he answered. "Weren't you listening? Miriam has an important interview for her article. She'll be out of town that night."

Dad took a bite of tomato with some kind of

leaves on it. "So," he explained, "I'll have to stay home to answer the door."

Whoa, I thought. This can't happen. No way.

"I'm sorry, Nick," said Miriam, sounding as though she meant it. "But we really need you to help out."

"C-c-can't he go with his friends?"

Dwayne stared at his plate. The truth smacked me like a fist. Dwayne didn't have friends.

This is so not fair. My friends will think I'm an idiot.

They all looked at me. Miriam tense. Dad expectant. Dwayne antsy. What could I say?

I couldn't say no. Miriam and Dwayne already thought I was Satan. Besides, Dad would make me do it anyway.

But I couldn't say yes, either. My friends would hate me. Worse. They'd laugh at me.

Whoever heard of dragging your brother along on Halloween? Wait . . . didn't Jeff bring his little brother last year? Yeah, but his brother's cool. Dwayne is about as cool as homework.

"What about his dad?" I said. "Couldn't he take him?"

Miriam and Dad exchanged nervous glances.

Dwayne's face turned redder than his hair. When his lower lip started to tremble, he bit it.

How come his face was always telling me way more than I wanted to hear?

"Yeah," I said, trying to sound nice. "He can come. It'll be fine."

Big Problem #2   10

Halloween, tonight. Me, stuck with Dwayne. Could life get worse? You bet.

Big problem number one was basketball. We did drills all week at practice. Killer drills. Make-you-want-to-throw-up-your-insides drills.

Thursday, we scrimmaged with the seventh and eighth grade team. Carson played point guard while I warmed the bench.

Coach wouldn't announce the starters until next week, but my chances were zero. I knew it. So why did I keep killing myself doing these stupid drills?

"It's not wasted," Miriam tried to console me. "It's heart healthy."

Like I cared.

I'm going to keep doing them, though. Call me stupid, but I'm not giving up.

Big problem number two was Halloween. I still hadn't told anyone that Dwayne was coming. Why? Because Tuesday, when I saw Derek in the hall, I wanted to tell him, but he said, "Hey, Nick, how's Duh-wayne?"

"Duh-usual," I said, and kept on walking.

Wednesday, Carson said, "Nick, I think I might go as a geek for Halloween. D'ya think Dwayne'll loan me his hair gel?"

Thursday, Josh said, "Dwayne's lucky. He's so weird he doesn't need a costume."

How could I tell them that weird, geeky, hair-gelled Duh-wayne was coming with us? Instead, I laughed at their jokes while little firebombs exploded in my gut. Friday I bought my first pack of Rolaids. I wasn't sure what acid indigestion was, but I was positive I had it.

So now it's Halloween, and I'm Lancelot—without the armored breastplate. I couldn't find another roasting pan anywhere. And the pie pan I cut up didn't look anything like a crown. King Arthur would have split his gussets laughing at it.

Serious thumps, bumps, and murmurs came from behind Dwayne's closed door as he and Miriam worked on his costume. I waited, fingering the

Rolaids pack in my pocket to be sure it was still there. I figured Dwayne would show up in one of those plastic costumes, as a Teletubby or something, but he surprised me.

"Ta da!" He bounded into the kitchen, so proud of himself. He wore one of Miriam's jackets—a long, red velvety tunic with puffy sleeves and a leather belt over it. Black tights covered his legs, along with her boots, which came up over his knees.

I figured he was supposed to be my squire, but he looked more like Puss-'n-Boots in too-big clothes.

Dwayne swept his arm out to one side and bowed. Then he raised up, his face suddenly tense. "Do you know what I am?" he asked.

"Sure," I said. "You're a squire."

The grin practically split his face.

I looked at Dwayne and sighed. I still hadn't told anyone he was coming.

We left Dad dishing out Tootsie Roll Pops and Rice Krispie Treats to Goldilocks, three bears, and a small freckled princess. Under my shield, I hid a pillowcase filled with toilet paper for rolling houses. Dwayne carried a plastic pumpkin.

What was it about Halloween that felt different from any other night? Something electric. Worried as I was, I could still feel it.

Every porch light in the neighborhood glowed. Some little kid in a Dracula costume cut across our front yard, giving last minute tips to a tiny witch. "The Jacksons have the biggest candy bars. . . . Stay away from the dog. . . ."

"Don't forget to say thank you!" shouted a dad from the sidewalk.

It took us five minutes to walk to Josh's house, Dwayne swinging his pumpkin, me counting the firebombs in my stomach, nobody saying much. Boy, I dreaded what was coming next.

Magic, Josh, and Derek waited in the front yard.

Magic stepped forward in a long black cape with stars all over it.

"Merlin," I said.

"At your service." He waved a black cardboard wand, the kind that comes in magic kits—only Magic had drawn cool designs on this one with a silver marker.

Behind him, Josh and Derek argued over whose red-and-yellow face paint looked the best. Both wore rainbow-colored clown wigs and big green bow ties. Except for a piece of Derek's curly hair sticking out, they could have been twins.

"Hey, Dwayne," said Magic.

Josh and Derek turned. "Dwayne?" they echoed at the same time.

"What's up?" said Dwayne, trying to sound cool.

"Prices," Magic answered.

Dwayne giggled like a two-year-old.

I winced. *Pop, pop.* Firebombs in my gut.

"Uh . . . what gives?" asked Carson, just walking up. He wore black leather pants and a black Harley t-shirt with a pack of Marlboros rolled up in the sleeve. "Dwayne's going with us," I answered casually, as if it were no big deal. *Pop, pop, pop.*

Carson motioned me closer with a jerk of his head. "You're kidding, right?"

"No such luck," I answered low, hoping Dwayne couldn't hear me. He was still giggling and bowing to Magic. "His mom's out of town. We're stuck."

"We?" said Carson.

Dwayne bounced over to us. "What's up?" He grinned at Carson and squirmed like he had to go to the bathroom.

Carson stared at him. "What *are* you?" he asked.

Dwayne's eyes danced with excitement. "Nick's

squire," he bragged. "Nick's square," Derek whispered too loud to Carson.

"Or squirt," said Josh.

All three of them laughed.

My stomach twisted like a wrung-out towel. Had Dwayne heard? I couldn't look. But I did.

Dwayne's eyes weren't dancing anymore. They were as still as glass.

A Better Idea

I wanted to go home, to forget how much I'd looked forward to being Lancelot, to eating candy, to hanging out.

Dwayne's eyes grew glassier, and wetter. He was going to cry, right here in front of everybody.

Carson crossed his arms over his chest and dared me with a cool stare.

My face pumped heat as fast as my palms poured sweat. What did he expect me to do?

Josh and Derek crossed their arms and glared, too. Tough guys in clown wigs. Man, did they look stupid.

"Good squire!" exclaimed Magic, throwing back his cape and aiming his magic wand at Dwayne. "I command thee to procure treats from yon cottage."

He jerked his head toward Josh's house, then winked at Dwayne.

Dwayne blinked back his tears, then looked to me for direction.

"Yeah, sure, go," I said, giving him a push toward the front porch. I fumbled in my pocket for a Rolaid. "But, hey," I called after him, "no candy corn."

"Are you nuts?" said Carson. "Candy corn is great."

"Yeah," said Derek. "I love candy corn."

Derek would love arsenic if Carson did, but at least their attention was off Dwayne. I mouthed a silent thank you to Magic.

After that, everyone ignored Dwayne and hauled in candy. The explosions in my gut eased up. Dwayne stayed quiet and followed us like a stray puppy. By 8:00 my sack had enough M&Ms, lollipops, and other good junk to last me a month.

"Hey," I said, reaching into my bag and pulling out two rolls of toilet paper. "Let's roll Ali's house."

"Nah," said Carson. "I've got a better idea."

"Yeah, what?" I asked. Carson always had better ideas.

He stopped under a streetlight and waited until

everyone circled him, even Dwayne. The same glow that spotlighted him threw our shadows out into the darkness. He motioned us closer.

"Satan's Circle," he hissed.

I laughed, figuring it for a joke.

"What about it?" whispered Derek.

"We're going to sit in it," said Carson.

"In the dark?" asked Josh, his voice jittery. "On Halloween?"

"Not me," said Magic.

"Me either," I echoed.

"You're crazy," muttered Josh.

"Yeah," breathed a faint voice.

Wow, even Derek thought Carson was nuts on this one.

"What's Satan's Circle?" whispered Dwayne.

"Shhh," I said, elbowing his shoulder. "I'll tell you later."

"Tell him now," said Carson. "Maybe *he'll* go. Maybe a dopey third grader . . . "

Dwayne shrank.

" . . . is braver than the rest of you wimps."

Dwayne stood tall again.

"Uh, it's a place," I explained, "a big circle, in a field, just outside of town. Nothing grows in it."

Dwayne's eyebrows wrinkled in thought.

Please, I prayed, oh, please, oh, please, don't explain photosynthesis—or suggest manure.

"And some people," Carson sneered, "think that anything you put in it will disappear." He laughed. "I wonder if anyone's ever put a squire in it."

Carson could be such a jerk.

"It's true," Josh swore. "My dad camped beside it when he was a kid. He left a flashlight in it, and the next morning it was gone."

"That's nothing," added Derek. "My grandmother said a whole cow vanished from it when she was thirteen."

"Yeah?" said Carson. "What's been lost lately?"

None of us could think of a thing. All the stories were old ones.

"Come on, guys," Carson urged. "It's just some old superstition. Let's do it."

Deep down, I knew the legend probably couldn't be true. But tossing toilet paper in Ali's trees sounded a lot better to me than sitting in a dark field in the middle of nowhere on Halloween night.

"Look," I said, "we can't get there and back by 9:30. Dwayne's got to be home then."

"So take him home now," said Carson.

"It's still too far," said Josh.

Derek nodded his head up and down like a busted robot.

Magic, of course, had disappeared.

"Wimps," muttered Carson. "Okay. So let's smoke. I've got a whole pack. Carson unrolled the Marlboros from his shirtsleeve. I should have known it wasn't a prop.

Coach's smoking rule might not matter to Carson, but it mattered to me. Still, anything sounded better than sitting in a spooky field named after Satan.

"Fine," I mumbled. Who'd know? Derek was the only one of us not on the team, and he'd never rat on Carson.

Something pulled my sleeve.

Dwayne. How could I have forgotten Dwayne?

He probably thought smoking was a federal crime. Either that, or one puff would kill us all, deader than a roomful of mummies.

Carson gave Dwayne a dirty look. Then he grinned.

"Don't worry," he said. "Dwayne won't tell." Carson mouthed the words slowly and evenly, as though each one might break. "Will you, Dwayne?"

Everyone turned toward Dwayne. He didn't look much like a squire anymore. He didn't even look like Puss-'n-Boots. He just looked like a scared little kid wearing his mother's clothes.

I wished *he* could disappear.

A Bad Idea 12

Would Dwayne tell on us if we smoked? Sure he would. I could see him and his heart-healthy mom planning an anti-tobacco program for my whole grade. "You guys go on," I said. "We'll catch up."

Carson, Derek, and Josh shrugged and headed for Josh's house. Two clowns and a biker. Laughing and shoving each other.

"Look," I said to Dwayne. "It's no big deal. Honest. Cigarettes won't kill you till you're old and have smoked a million." That was probably stretching the truth. Still, I was pretty sure one couldn't hurt.

"Besides, I'm only going to have one—just to take Carson's mind off his other stupid idea."

Dwayne dug the toe of his mom's boot into the grass. "Okay," he squeaked in his mouse voice.

I didn't know whether to hate him or feel sorry for him. Mostly I decided to feel sorry for me.

By the time we got to Josh's house, I had a plan. I knew where they'd smoke—Josh's tree house. If Dwayne didn't actually see us smoke, we could deny it.

"Dwayne," I said. "You've been a great squire. Now I need you to be a great sentry."

I led him to the base of the tree and presented him with my sword, holding it out flat with both hands. The light from the opening in the tree house hit the plastic blade, making it shine like a real one.

"Thanks, Nick." He grasped the hilt with both hands and grinned as if I'd knighted him. Timidly, he stabbed the night air.

"Nice form. Now, you stay here and whistle three times if you hear anyone coming. Okay?"

Dwayne lowered the sword. "I can't whistle," he whispered.

"Then cough three times. Okay?"

"Okay." He smiled again. He honestly thought I'd given him an important job.

My fingers gripped a board nailed partway up the tree, and I pulled myself up. Just before crawling through the hole into the tree house, I glanced down at Dwayne. If being alone scared him, he didn't show it.

He huddled against the trunk, watching me, hugging the sword with both arms wrapped around his body for warmth. Then he unwrapped one arm and gave me a thumbs-up.

I scrambled into the tree house, feeling nothing at all like Lancelot.

"Hi, guys," I muttered. "What's up?"

"Us, you dummy," said Magic.

So, Magic was back. Why not? If we got caught, *poof!* He'd be gone.

The lantern on the floor gave off enough light so that I could see Carson's face.

"Where's Dwayne?" he asked. He locked his fingers behind his head and leaned against a poster of Darth Vader.

Other than the lantern and a plastic crate filled with comics, the room was pretty bare—except for the walls. Josh had them covered with posters of old action movies. *Indiana Jones, Star Wars, Batman, Jaws.* He collected them. *Jaws* was his favorite.

"Dwayne," I bragged, "is guarding the entrance."

"No good," said Carson. "Get him up here."

"What!" I yelled, then lowered my voice to

a whisper. "You've wanted him gone all night, remember? Besides, he'd rat on us."

"Yeah," Josh agreed.

"He'd tell," echoed Derek.

"He would," said Magic.

"Call him," said Carson. "I've got an idea."

"What's wrong with *my* idea?"

"I've got a better one," said Carson.

It was all I could do not to hit him. "Yeah? Like what?"

"You'll see," said Carson, smiling confidently. "Trust me."

That won Derek.

Magic and Josh muttered, "This better be good."

I glanced at my watch. 8:30. Carson had a whole hour for his plan. I wished there were enough light for me to read the label on my Rolaids. Can you overdose on antacids?

I should have gone home. Instead, I leaned through the opening.

"Dwayne," I called. "Come on up."

He bumped and thumped up the ladder, working hard not to drop the sword. I reached down and pulled him in.

Dwayne rubbed his eyes. "Wow!" he exclaimed, "terrific posters."

"Thanks," said Josh.

"Have a smoke," said Carson, handing Dwayne a lighted cigarette.

"No, thank you," Dwayne answered firmly.

"Are you crazy?" I shouted at Carson. "He's a little kid!"

"He's a little kid who won't tell on us if he's done it, too," said Carson smugly.

Oh.

"Good idea!" Derek slapped his thigh in admiration.

"I won't tell," said Dwayne quietly.

"Maybe, maybe not," said Carson. "But this would clinch it. Besides, it'll make you one of us," he lied. "Go on, take a drag."

Dwayne looked to me for help. He held the cigarette with two hands, far away, as if it were a poisonous snake.

"Just do it," I advised. "It won't kill you. I promise."

Dwayne pulled the cigarette toward his face, still using both hands. He held it like you'd play a clarinet. I watched the end glow as he sucked on it.

"Don't inhale," I warned.

Too late.

He'd already breathed in with a giant wheeze that exploded back out of him as if his insides were coming up. I'd never seen so much smoke. His eyes began to water. He dropped the cigarette.

Josh, Carson, and Derek were laughing their heads off. I lunged forward to grab the hot cigarette before it rolled through the floor opening. Magic reached behind Dwayne to pound his back.

Dwayne forced a fake smile, then he threw up. Projectile. Chunks of Halloween candy mixed with Miriam's cooking—shrimp and spinach linguine. Chocolate, pink, and green. Smelly. Slimy. On me.

Dwayne covered his mouth with both hands, trying to hold back the next gush.

I dove to the floor and watched the second batch of puke shoot past me. *Splat!* Dead center onto the *Jaws* poster.

Josh stopped laughing.

Dwayne sat cross-legged on the floor, dazed. Slowly, he lifted his arm to wipe his mouth, then froze. He couldn't smear barf on his mother's velvet tunic.

I sat up and stared down at my soaked shirt. Me, Lancelot, wishing I'd worn a breastplate. I choked back a gag.

Josh gaped helplessly at his slimed poster. Derek, Carson, even Magic rolled on the floor laughing—at me.

I couldn't decide which was worse, the feel of all that still-warm puke seeping through my shirt, the sour smell of shrimp-vomit, or them laughing.

"You moron!" I shouted at Dwayne.

Magic stifled a snicker, but Derek and Carson howled even louder. Dwayne hiccupped twice, then began to whimper.

I hated all five of them.

Way Too Hard 13

Halloween taught me a lot.

    1. Get your candy and go home.

    2. Wear something waterproof.

    3. Don't inhale.

Those were the easy lessons.

I felt I'd learned something bigger, too, only I couldn't quite figure out what. It was all mixed up with how I felt about Dwayne—a real loser, but he meant well. And how I felt about my friends—complete jerks, but still, my friends. And how I felt about me—terrible.

After Dwayne emptied his guts all over me and the shark, I bolted from the tree house, found the closest garden hose, and washed my shirt. The air was crisp, but not too cold if I'd been dry. Wet, I'd shivered all the way home.

Dwayne followed me, whimpering like a baby. I couldn't look at him. He'd ruined Halloween. And I knew, whether he meant to or not, he would go on ruining things.

Our porch light was off—Dad's signal that the house was now closed to trick-or-treaters. We slipped quietly through the front door, hoping he wouldn't get a whiff of my smelly shirt or notice Dwayne's tear-and-barf-streaked face.

"How was everything?" he asked, never glancing up from his ten-pound book.

"Fine," we lied.

"That's good," he called as we took off up the stairs. "Don't forget to brush your teeth."

"Nuh-nick-ick," Dwayne hiccupped as I turned into my room, "I'm suh-ick-sorry."

I slammed my door.

Suddenly I knew why knighthood had been dead so long. Chivalry. Honor. They were both way too hard.

Sunday, I would have found a way to stay out of the house, even if it had rained javelins. Luckily it was warm and sunny.

I spent all day in the driveway shooting baskets,

dribbling, not returning phone calls. I didn't want to talk to anyone, not even Magic. How could he laugh at me? *I* didn't puke.

Last night, I'd scrubbed my skin raw in the shower, but I could still smell it. Barf body. Ham hair. At this rate, I wouldn't have a single friend by Thanksgiving.

Okay, I told myself, save what you learned. Otherwise, delete Halloween. Picture yourself as a point guard. Perfect passes, awesome assists, total ball control.

Nick Kimble drives the lane and fakes everyone out with a reverse lay-up. What a move! Cheering fans. Yes! A star.

I pumped my fist, then pounded the ball hard into the pavement. Stepping behind the three-point chalk mark, I squared my shoulders, bent my knees, and eyed the back of the rim. I released the ball with my arm, wrist, and fingers fully extended.

Swish.

Yes!

"Good shot." The puny voice drifted in from behind me.

I whirled around. Dwayne—wearing shorts he must have outgrown when he was four. Penelope—

rubbing and circling his white sneakers and pulled-up socks. Me—staring at the top of his carved-in-redwood hair. It made me mad all over again.

"Okay if I watch?" he asked, barely lifting his head. He looked like a dog who'd just peed on the carpet.

"Get your own friends," I snapped. "Get a life."

I heaved the ball into the carport. *Blam!* It slammed into the garbage cans. Penelope pounced on it, making me feel stupid.

Only a minute ago, I'd felt good about myself.

"Dinner's ready," called Dad.

Dinner, I thought. Weird food. Me looking across the table at Dwayne's hair.

Dad ruffled Dwayne's hair, then mine, as we filed past him. Dwayne combed his hair back into place with his fingers.

I slipped into my chair as Miriam brought in a platter of fish covered with green stuff swimming in sauce. Seafood. Memories of shrimp-vomit. The smell sent an SOS straight to my stomach. Breakfast and lunch churned and shot halfway up my throat.

"Excuse me," I burped, pushing my chair back. I covered my mouth and bolted for the bathroom.

Vomit Victim 14

Monday morning I woke up wanting to skip school, to tell everyone I was sick. After all, I had barfed at dinner last night.

But if I stayed home, I'd miss basketball practice, and Coach was naming the starters. I sure didn't want to hear that I hadn't made it from my friends. I wasn't even sure they were my friends.

So I braced myself for being tagged vomit-victim and headed for school. It started as soon as I got on the bus. Two girls I didn't even know held their noses and snickered.

I slid into the first seat, the one right across from the driver. Nobody ever sits that far up, which was okay by me.

Words bounced back and forth across the aisles. Words and laughter. Shrieks of laughter, actually.

Dwayne . . . puked . . . Nick . . . (shriek). . . .No!
. . .Yes! . . .Noodles . . . (another shriek) . . . you're
kidding! . . .Green ones . . . (major shrieks) . . . soooo
gross . . . you wouldn't believe . . . everywhere . . .
(shriek, shriek) . . . slimed. . . .

All morning, I tried to ignore the lame jokes
and laughter. I don't know if I succeeded on
the outside, but inside I was definitely ballistic. Totally manic. Grinding-my-teeth, clinching-my-fists
psycho.

At lunchtime, I gave myself a pep talk. Nick . . .
get a grip. Act like it's no big deal.

I took a deep breath and strolled casually into the
cafeteria. Magic sat at a corner table with Derek and
Carson. He was waving his arms all around, telling
some crazy story about bat attacks.

Please, guys, I pleaded silently, skip the vomit
jokes. I took another deep breath and plopped
myself down.

"What's up?" I said, faking my most convincing
I'm-cool-nothing-bothers-me attitude.

"Chuck," said Magic.

"Chuck?" I didn't get it.

Carson and Derek howled.

Then I got it. *Upchuck.*

My face flamed up faster than a gasoline torch.

I ripped open my lunch bag. "Funny," I muttered. "Real funny."

"Hey, I'm sorry," said Magic. "But, come on. It *was* funny."

I couldn't even look at him.

"So," said Magic to nobody in particular. "When's Coach going to announce the starters? Before practice, or after?"

"Who cares?" said Carson. "I won't be there."

What? I thought. Carson's going to miss his moment of glory?

"You're kidding," said Magic.

"I wish." Carson rolled his eyes. "Derek and I have to be at Ali's by 3:30 to clean up the mess."

Ali's? I thought. What mess?

As if on cue, Ali walked by our table and flashed Carson a huge grin. She looked like Britney Spears when she smiled.

"See you this afternoon," she called.

Carson grinned back, pointing toward her like a basketball player acknowledging an assist.

"Her dad found out we rolled her house on Halloween," Derek bragged.

They rolled Ali's house?! When? After I left? My face had been hot before, but now it burned out of control.

I crumpled my lunch bag in my fist, sandwich and all. I stormed out, slamming the smashed bag into the closest garbage container. A perfect slam dunk. I wish it had been Carson's head.

I slouched in math class, trying to multiply decimals. A moving picture of Carson's smug mouth saying "I've got a better idea" replayed in my brain. As if my idea of rolling Ali's house was the dumbest thing he'd ever heard. And then he went and did it without me?!

I erased my last math problem, rubbing the paper so hard it tore.

Magic's mouth joined Carson's in my head. "What's up? Chuck." Suddenly dozens of mouths chimed in. "Slimed!" shouted half the bus. "Shriek!" screamed the other half. Before I knew it, everybody was in my brain. Dad, Miriam, Dwayne, Coach. Everybody. "What did you learn in school today?" "Let's all play." "Time out." "Suicide sprints."

Then I started getting reruns. "Slimed—Upchuck—Better idea."

Blam! I slammed my fist on the desk. The whole class turned and stared. Mrs. Morton raised an eyebrow.

"Sorry," I mumbled.

•   •   •

Social Studies. Last period. Finally. We were reading the Declaration of Independence. "Our lives, our fortunes, and our sacred honor" jumped out of the text. Usually I would have wanted to discuss that, but not today.

Twenty-eight minutes until basketball practice. The rotten end to a rotten day. I knew I wouldn't be a starter. So why was my stomach flipping like fifty fast-food burgers. Was it because I hadn't had any lunch, or because deep down, I thought I had a chance?

What about Carson? He'd be missing—without an excuse. What had Coach said? Anyone, and I mean *anyone*, who misses a practice without an excuse won't play in the next game.

Our first game was Wednesday. The day after tomorrow. Maybe I did have a chance.

I'd know soon. I'd know in twenty-six and a half minutes.

The Starters 15

It's usually easy to go unnoticed in the chaos of the locker room. I hoped so. I didn't need to be the target of any more vomit jokes. I buried my head inside my locker and pretended to look for something. The smell drove me back out. So I left the door open and tried to disappear behind it. Magic could have done this without a problem.

I pulled out the Snickers bar I'd bought from Norman after class. "Norman" is what we call the vending machine, after the crazy guy in *Psycho*— because you never know what it might do.

Eating before running sprints was probably a dumb idea, but I had to eat something. I was starving.

Rustle. Crackle. Crinkle. Crinkle. Why do candy wrappers make so much noise?

"He was so mad," said Magic, peeling off his jeans to change into gym shorts.

"Major rage," said Josh, rummaging through his duffel. "You should have seen him."

Come on, I thought. How long am I going to be news? Wait. Josh wasn't even at lunch. Was he?

"If my mother'd done that, I'd kill her," said Magic.

Huh? My mother? Did he mean Miriam?

"*He* ought to die for telling her," said Josh. "I bet Coach makes us run extra suicide sprints."

"Sprints?" I said, forgetting I was hiding. "Who's got to run extra sprints?"

"You, me, probably everybody," said Magic.

"Coach just talked to Paul," explained Josh. "His no-brained mother called over the weekend to complain. Her *precious* boy—"

Josh paused to pose on tiptoe and flap his arms like a ballerina.

"—is having to work too hard at practice."

I groaned. Didn't all parents know not to do something that stupid? I bet even Miriam knew. Poor Paul.

At least they weren't laughing at me anymore.

I looked up at the wall clock. Forty-five seconds and counting.

•　•　•

"Okay, guys, have a seat." Coach stood in front of the bleachers, impatiently tapping his clipboard against his pants.

We all climbed over the first rows and spread out across the top ones. Magic slid in next to me. I ignored him.

"You still mad?" he whispered.

I shrugged. I was angrier at Carson—for stealing my idea. Was I still mad at Magic? Yeah. A little.

"I said I was sorry, okay?" Magic elbowed my arm. "And I'm sorry I laughed at you on Halloween."

I shrugged again. All I cared about hearing right now was who the starters were.

"Come on," he persisted. "You would have laughed if it had been me." Magic started chuckling all over again. "You should have seen yourself."

"Quiet!" shouted Coach. "We've got a game Wednesday and this is our last practice, so it needs to be good. But first, I've got some things to go over."

This is it, I thought. He's announcing the starters. My heart pounded all the way up in my throat.

"First," he said, "I hear that some of you think practice is too hard."

All eyes cut toward Paul, who was trying to look smaller.

"I've got two things to say about that. One. . ."
—Coach held up one finger. "our practices *have*
been tough. That's why I told every one of you that
I needed commitment. Two. . ."— he held up two
fingers "anyone who has a problem comes to me
about it. *Don't*" —Coach grinned the Grinch-
grin— "send your mother."

Paul's head drooped practically to his waist as he
shrank another two sizes.

"Second," said Coach, "I want to tell all of you
what a great job you're doing."

Second? He already did two. Or was that the second thing under the first thing? And why was the
man always counting?

"I wish you could all be starters," he continued.

Finally, I thought, he's going to tell us who. My
palms started to sweat.

"You boys watch college and pro ball. The guys
on the bench are just as important as the starters.
Their big job comes at practice—giving the first
team good, solid competition."

Oh, right, I thought, glancing around to see if
anyone was buying the it's-an-honor-to-be-on-the-
bench speech. Josh rolled his eyes. Magic's left leg
pumped up and down like a piston.

Announce the starters! I thought.

"Maybe he's going to announce the bench first," somebody said in a low voice. "You know, like the Miss America runners-up."

Everybody laughed.

"Quiet!" yelled Coach. "Now," he said softly, raising his clipboard, "for the third thing."

Good grief, I thought. This isn't math. Stop counting. I can't stand this.

"I'm going to read the names of the starters."

My heart stopped. The gym got so quiet, I could hear cars going by way out on the road.

"But first . . . "

I wanted to scream. A bunch of guys groaned.

"Let me remind everybody that I could make some changes down the road, so all you guys keep working hard."

Now. Please. Announce them now.

"Magic," said Coach. "I want you to start at center."

"Yes!" Magic mouthed under his breath.

Mad or not, I felt a shiver of excitement for him. I gave him a thumbs-up.

"Ross and Scotty, you two will play at the forward positions."

Shoot, I thought. That means Josh didn't make it.

"The number two guard will be Paul."

Paul, who had shrunk to the size of a Munchkin, suddenly grew two feet right where he sat. I could have sworn I saw Coach wink at him.

"Point guard . . ." said Coach.

I held my breath.

"Nick . . ."

My heart leaped right out of my chest.

"I want you to play point guard in practice today, but Carson will start Wednesday when he gets back from his uncle's funeral."

The Honor Code's a Joke   16

What did you learn in school today?" Dad asked, the second I sat down to dinner.

"Honor sucks!" I shouted, stabbing a cheese tortellini like it was Carson's heart.

"Nicholas!" Dad barked.

Miriam stared at me. Dwayne gaped.

"Sorry," I muttered.

"You should be," said Dad.

"What's wrong?" Miriam asked, reaching across the table to touch my arm.

I jerked it away. "Nothing." I jabbed some more tortellini. I looked up. They were all staring at me, probably wondering why I was attacking helpless pieces of pasta.

"Are you having a problem with your girlfriend?" Miriam asked cautiously.

"My girlfriend?"

"Isn't Lucy your girlfriend?" said Miriam.

"Lucy?" I echoed dumbly. Who the heck was Lucy?

"Nick, please don't misunderstand," she said. "I don't mean to pry into your personal life . . . but . . . well . . . I mean . . . you *do* have her initials all over your notebook."

"Huh?"

"L.B.D.," she said. "Lucy Davis. Isn't she in your class?"

"Lucy Davis? Yeah, but . . ." Then it hit me. L.B.D. Life Before Dwayne. It was all over my notebook. It was all over everything.

The three of them waited expectantly for me to explain L.B.D. What could I say?

"It doesn't stand for Lucy," I replied lamely.

Before Miriam could ask what it did stand for, I muttered, "I'm not upset about a girl. It's about honor. The honor code's a joke."

And then, before I knew it, I was telling them everything, the whole rotten story. How Carson had lied to Coach. And Coach believed him. His uncle's funeral! I bet he doesn't even have an uncle.

"That's not fair," said Dwayne.

"No, it's not," Dad agreed. "But, Nick, doesn't the

honor code also mean you're on your honor to report someone who breaks it?"

"Yeah, sort of, but, Dad, *nobody* does that. I'd lose all my friends if I did that."

"I wouldn't," said Miriam. "I'd love to tell your coach what Carson did." Her face had the same Grinch-like gleam as Coach's.

"No!" I shouted. "That's even worse." And to think, I thought she'd know better.

"Well, at least let me report your coach to the principal. The nerve of him" —Miriam swelled up and squared her shoulders— "calling *your* name when he named the starters, only to tell you that you *wouldn't* be one of them. How does anyone that insensitive get—"

"Pleeeeze," I pleaded, "don't do anything. I'll handle it. Okay?"

Miriam looked hard at me, then at Dad. He nodded.

"Okay," she mumbled, but I could tell her heart wasn't in it.

After dinner I lay on my bed, thinking and talking to Sir Kay while I rubbed his worn-out ear. My best friend's a bear, I thought, embarrassed by the plain truth of it.

"Honor's a big deal to me," I said. "Am I crazy?"

Sir Kay didn't answer.

I rolled over on my side and came face-to-face with Mom smiling out from her picture frame. What would Mom say? I bet she'd be mad at Coach, just like Miriam. And disappointed in Carson, just like me. I also bet she'd hug me and say she was proud I wanted to handle it myself.

So how would I handle it?

"Maybe Carson will break a leg," I said.

Sir Kay raised an eyebrow, I swear.

"Okay, okay," I muttered. "That wasn't an honorable thought."

But today, honor sounded like a pretty ancient word to me. I wasn't at all sure it mattered anymore.

After that things got crazier. And worse.

It started at school the next day. Mostly the day was long and boring, except for watching Carson and Ali eating lunch together. Alone. Grinning at each other like a couple of idiots. Nobody seemed to care that Carson had lied. They acted like he was a hero for having so much nerve.

In Social Studies, I kept my mouth shut. We did end up discussing the part where the Declaration of Independence signers pledged their lives, their fortunes, and their sacred honor. We talked about what it meant *then*. It didn't occur to anyone that it meant something *now*.

After school, Magic and I decided to shoot some baskets on the outdoor court. I figured I had bigger things to stay mad about than Magic's laughing because I'd been puked on. Besides, he was probably right. If I'd seen all six skinny feet of him covered in barf, I'd have laughed too.

I was feeding the ball to him under the basket when Coach yelled, "Nick! Can I see you?"

"Sure." I tossed the ball to Magic and trotted over to where Coach stood. Maybe he found out Carson didn't have an uncle. Maybe I was the new point guard.

"Yes, sir?"

"Perhaps you weren't listening yesterday," he practically hissed at me. "I told you boys to come to me if you had complaints. Right? No family members with good intentions. Remember?"

"Yes, sir," I said, a cold, panicky feeling seizing my gut. What had Miriam done?

"So how is it, when we haven't even played a game yet, you think the bench should have more playing time?"

"Huh?" I answered like a total moron.

"Michael Jordan." Coach sneered. "So you think I need a lecture on Michael Jordan being cut from his high school team, all because some coach probably didn't give him enough playing time?"

"What!" I exclaimed. "Coach, I never—"

"It just so happens," he cut me off, "that I care what you think. And I'll listen to what you think. Even if it's some harebrained theory about Michael—"

"But, Coach—" I tried to explain.

"Do you think you're Michael Jordan?"

"No, of course not. I never—"

"Good," he said. "But whatever you think, I'd appreciate hearing it from you. That's how a team works. Your family's not on my team. You are. Understand?"

"Yes, sir."

"Good. You're a hard worker, Nick. I like that." He turned and walked away.

I couldn't believe it. Miriam! How could she have done this to me?

For ten minutes, I was too mad to speak.

Magic, when I finally told him, actually tried to defend her.

"Nick," he argued, "Miriam promised you she wouldn't rat on Carson, or go to the principal. She never said she wouldn't—"

"Oh, please," I said. "I can't believe she's that dumb. *Anyone* knows."

"She's used to Dwayne," said Magic.

That stopped me. He was right. She probably ran to teachers all the time, because Dwayne needed all the help he could get.

Well, *I* didn't. Couldn't she see that?

When Magic's mom dropped me at home, the first thing I spotted was Dwayne, sitting cross-legged in the grass, stroking Penelope.

"Hi, Nick," he called.

"Your mother needs a brain transplant!" I snapped. "She went to my coach. Do you know how dumb that is? It's dumber than dumb. I hate her!"

Dwayne's puny little fist squeezed a handful of Penelope's hair, while two fat tears rolled down his cheeks.

I stormed into the house.

A neon-green Post-it note greeted me in the kitchen. "*We'll be late. Dinner is in the fridge*" was dashed off in Miriam's loopy handwriting. Yes! I thought. I don't have to face her yet.

What could I say? Thanks for trying to help, but you've made my life stink worse than sewage? Or how about, I'm beginning to like your weird food, but please take it and Dwayne and go back to your home planet?

I microwaved my dinner and went straight to my room. I stuck a note on my door:

Gone to bed early

DO NOT DISTURB

Then I slammed it.

Sir Kay and Mom both looked at me. "Dwayne is outside crying," they said.

I turned Mom's picture down and jammed Sir Kay's face into the pillow.

"Tomorrow," I fired back at them. "I'll tell him I'm sorry tomorrow."

The next morning Miriam burst into my room like a crazy person. She clutched a piece of paper.

"Where's Dwayne?" she demanded.

"Huh?" I mumbled. "Is it time to get up?" I looked at my alarm clock. I had twenty more minutes to sleep.

Miriam sat down on my bed and shook me. "Where's Dwayne?" she repeated.

"In his room?" I asked. "The bathroom?"

"No," she said. "The only thing in his room was this note." She waved a sheet of notebook paper in my face.

I propped myself up on one elbow and read:

DON'T WORRY. I'LL BE BACK.

in neat bold print.

"Nick," she pleaded, "what do you know about this? Be back when? Where did he go?"

The truth woke me up. It was like a police siren going off in my head.

Dwayne had run away.

Totally Gruesome 17

Dwayne. Gone.

My head woke up faster than my body. My hand drooped numb where I'd slept on it. When I shook it, tiny needles shot up through my fingertips.

Had Dwayne really run away? Because I hated his mother?

My feet tangled in the sheets, jerking, trying to get out of bed. Miriam paced, rereading Dwayne's message.

Dad padded into the room, half shaved. "Anything wrong?"

Miriam handed him the note. As he read it, his forehead scrunched and his eyebrows twisted.

"Nick." Dad looked up at me. "What do you know about this?"

So I told him. And Miriam. Everything. Except the part about hating her.

Dad looked at Miriam, confused. "You went to Nick's coach?"

She squinted as if she were trying to see through fog. "What?"

"Nick's coach," Dad repeated. "Did you talk to Nick's coach?"

"No." She slumped onto the side of my bed and stared up at him. "I didn't."

What? I thought. Didn't Coach say, don't send your mom to me? Something about moms with good intentions. No . . . wait. Family members. That's it. He said family members.

"Oh, no," I whispered.

"What?" Miriam squeezed my arm.

"Family members. He said no family members, and I thought he meant you, Miriam. But, no . . . don't you see? He must have meant Dwayne. So when I told Dwayne how stupid," I hesitated, remembering his face, "and that I hated—"

"Nick," said Miriam. "What are you saying? That *Dwayne* talked to your coach about your wanting playing time?"

"Yeah." I slowly untangled my feet, sat up on the side of my bed, and stared blankly at the floor. Sir Kay sprawled next to my bare feet. The corner of an empty Oreos package stuck out from under the bed.

"My God," Miriam moaned, swaying like she'd been zapped with a stun gun.

Dad blinked rapidly, unaware of the shaving cream dried onto half his face.

"Where would he go?" Miriam wondered aloud.

Dad came out of his trance. "Look," he said in his I'll-fix-everything voice. "We'll find him. Think. He feels as though he's let Nick down, and his feelings are hurt."

"Would he go to his dad's?" I asked.

Miriam turned on me like a pit bull. "He hates him!" she shouted.

"Dwayne hates his dad?" I asked quietly.

"No!" Miriam choked back a sob. "*He* hates Dwayne. A baby, he calls him. A wimp. Sometimes I'm afraid that Dwayne thinks that's why his father—"

She stopped.

Why his father what? I thought. Why he left? No. Maybe. I tried to imagine my own father calling me a baby and a wimp. I groaned. Isn't that what I'd called Dwayne?

"He was asleep when we got home last night," Dad said, "so he must have left early this morning. He can't have gotten far. Miriam, you drive through the neighborhood south of Sutton Street. I'll drive north."

"I'll go with you," I said.

"No." Dad grabbed one of my towels off the floor and wiped the shaving cream off his face. "Get ready for school. Your bus will be here soon."

"But, Dad," I protested, "it's my fault he's—"

Dad was already out the door, with Miriam right behind him.

I brushed my teeth and dressed. They'll be right back, I assured myself. Dwayne will be with them. Any second, they will all come through the door.

Meanwhile, I needed to do something, so I wandered into Dwayne's room looking for clues. I thought I'd stumbled into the wrong house. It didn't look anything like our old guest room.

The first thing I saw was a big shelf with plants all over it. Tall plants, tiny plants, weird plants. A cactus so shaggy it needed a haircut. Something else that looked like little green pitchers growing in a pot.

Next to that sat a giant red spike growing out of a flower bulb that wasn't even in dirt.

I crossed the room to get a closer look. The pitcher-looking plants actually held water, but they weren't cute. No, they had bloodred veins that could have been in a horror movie. Totally gruesome.

Next to them sat a pot full of green pods with sharp teeth that gaped open like little animal traps. I touched one.

"Yike!" I jumped. I swear, the stupid plant bit me.

Picking up a pencil, I carefully touched another one. It sprang shut. How creepy, I thought. And how cool.

I glanced around. A desk. A PC. Lots of stuffed animals. One neatly made bed. On top of a bookcase sat an awesome geometric sphere made of dozens of rods held together with black elastic. Did Dwayne build that?

The best thing of all sat on a small table in the corner. A chess set with carved playing pieces. Castles and kings and queens and knights—just like King Arthur, Guinevere, and their court, all lined up on the squares of a shiny castle floor.

Why hadn't I ever been in Dwayne's room before?

The answer stung me like a slap.

I strained to hear Dad's car pulling into the carport. Or Miriam's. Or Dwayne running up the stairs. Instead, I heard my school bus squeaking to a stop two blocks away.

Some Friend **18**

By second period, I'd quit worrying about Dwayne. Dad probably dragged him home two seconds after I jumped on the bus. Besides, Dwayne's note did say don't worry. And it said he'd be back.

On the way to math class, I passed Ali as she closed her locker.

"Hi, Nick."

"Hey," I answered. "You going to math?"

"In a minute," she said, sliding a spiral into her book bag. "I'm waiting for Carson."

"Yeah, well, see you there," I mumbled.

Then I remembered. Our first game. Today. How could I have forgotten? I'd also forgotten to tell Dad. Even if I only played a minute, I wanted him to come.

At lunch, I dialed the newspaper office. He was out. I tried home. Dad answered.

"Dad," I said, "today's our first—"

"Nick," he interrupted, "thanks for calling. We haven't found him. Don't worry. I'm sure he's fine." Dad was talking really fast.

"Miriam's pretty upset, though. Ever since she did that article on runaways—"

"Miriam did an article on runaways?"

"Sure," said Dad, "you remember. That's why she was out of town on Halloween. She told us about it at dinner. Remember? Anyway, she knows so much. All the scary things that can happen to those kids."

I didn't remember her even mentioning it.

"He's not at school." Dad talked even faster now. "We checked. Scoured the neighborhood. No luck. Miriam's driving around. I'm manning the phone. Better hang up."

Dad. Firing short sentences at me. He didn't sound like Dad.

"Don't worry, Nick. He'll turn up. Check back in an hour."

"Dad, what can I—"

Click.

I hung the receiver back on the pay phone and dragged down the hall to lunch. *They hadn't found Dwayne.* I couldn't believe it.

I slid into a lunch table across from Magic. He was busy peeling the top off a chocolate pudding container. Suddenly his mouth stretched open in a yawn so big I could practically see his breakfast.

"You're not going to believe this," I said.

"B'lev wha'?" he said, still yawning.

"Dwayne ran away."

His mouth snapped shut.

I told him everything—except about Dwayne's dad. I figured Dwayne would want that part to stay private.

Magic's jaw dropped halfway into his pudding cup when I said Dwayne had gone to Coach. But a minute or two later, his eyes kind of glazed over. He rested his chin in his hands. Was he listening or not?

"What a mess," he said when I finished.

"Where do you think he is?" I asked.

Magic thought a minute. "I wouldn't worry," he finally answered. "Nick, I'm sorry, but I gotta go. Keep me posted."

I watched him walk away. Some friend, I thought.

"What's his problem?" I grumbled.

"Whose problem?" asked Josh, plopping down in the seat Magic had left.

"Magic," I answered. "He's about as tuned in as a dead battery."

Josh shrugged. "Maybe his parents kept him awake all night."

"Huh?"

"His parents. You know. They fight a lot."

"Oh," I said. "Yeah."

"I figure that's why he splits all the time, don't you?" Josh opened a bag of chips and stuffed a fistful into his mouth.

"Huh?"

"Whenever there's trouble," Josh said with his mouth full. "You know, a conflict. Magic takes off. He gets enough of it at home, I guess."

Stunned, I watched Josh cram another handful of chips in his mouth. Why hadn't I ever thought of that?

I called home after lunch. No Dwayne.

This was stupid. Where could he be? I thought about all the places he went—which was zero. Dwayne never went anywhere. Except the kitchen to cook, or his room. The room I'd never been in. A few neighbors' houses on Halloween.

Halloween! It hit me like a brick. Josh's tree

house! Dwayne was hiding in Josh's tree house. The little creep was going to sit up there and read comics until everybody worried themselves extinct, and then he'd show up for dinner and get hugged silly by Dad and Miriam.

I sprinted for the phone to tell Dad. The answering machine clicked in. "You've reached the Kimbles. Please leave a message at the sound of—"

I slammed the receiver back on the hook. I just talked to him. Where had he gone?

If I went to get Dwayne, I'd miss my game. No way I was doing that. Finding lost brothers wasn't on Coach's list of excuses. Besides, I didn't want Coach to even know about this mess.

I couldn't miss my game. What if I went *after* the game?

I pictured Miriam driving around in circles, thinking about runaways getting knifed in dark alleys, or becoming heroin addicts.

I punched the side of the phone with my fist.

Normal Life 19

Our first game. I couldn't believe I was missing it—to rescue Dwayne. I must be crazy.

After I'd hung up the phone, I'd run to catch the school bus that went to Josh's house. What choice did I have? To play ball while my family was coming unglued?

At Josh's house, I hopped off the bus, then crept down the side yard so Dwayne wouldn't hear me and take off. The only running I'd planned to do was on the basketball court.

I ducked under the tree house and quickly scrambled up the ladder. I stuck my head up through the floor.

"Dwayne, it's me, Nick."

Silence.

I waited for my eyes to adjust to the dark. The

crate of comics came into view in the corner. It looked as though the barf had been cleaned up, but the smell lingered.

I could make out Darth Vader and Indiana Jones guarding the walls. *Jaws* loomed up out of the blackness, but he was sort of puckered where Dwayne had puked on him.

"Dwayne?"

No answer. No Dwayne.

I felt as though I'd been punched. I was so sure he'd be here.

The comic books were piled in a messy heap. Tarzan sprawled on top with the cover bent under. If Dwayne had been here they'd be stacked, neatly.

I grabbed a bunch off the top and flung them against the wall. "I hope he stays gone!" I shouted. I'd missed my game for nothing.

I walked home, kicking every pebble in sight. One skidded across the street and down a storm drain. Dwayne wouldn't hide somewhere dangerous, like a storm pipe. Would he?

When I turned onto my street, the first thing I saw was the police car parked in front of our house. My chest tightened as if it had been shrunk. I ran the rest of the way.

Dad sat on the sofa in the den, leaning forward

with his hands clasped. The cop sat across from him, writing something in a notebook spread out on the coffee table. A uniformed police officer. Sitting in my house. I felt like I was in a movie.

"Nick." Dad waved me into the room. "This is Officer Neal. Have a seat. We'll be through in a second."

"D-dwayne?" I asked, his name catching in my throat.

"No word yet," said Dad with phony cheerfulness. "But Officer Neal says not to worry. Runaway eight-year-olds almost always show up for dinner."

"Any ideas where your brother might be?" said the officer.

"No, sir," I said. "None."

He closed his notebook, shook Dad's hand, then said it was nice to meet me. Dad walked him out to his squad car.

"Dad," I said, as soon as he came back in. "The police?"

"It doesn't mean anything bad," he assured me. "It just gives us more people to look for him."

"Oh," I said, having trouble shaking the picture of a cop sitting in my den.

"Miriam has gone to Statesville," Dad continued. "That's where Dwayne's father lives, but apparently he's out of town. We don't honestly think Dwayne would go to him, but she should be there, just in case. The bus station hasn't seen him, but there's always the possibility he hitched a ride from someone on the highway."

I tried to imagine Dwayne hitchhiking. A puny little kid standing on the interstate in his creased pants and clean sneakers. Wouldn't someone just buy him an ice-cream cone and drive him home?

Dad must have read my mind, because he said, "I doubt anyone would pick up a small child without bringing him home, but Dwayne's so little he could stow away in a big truck stopped at a service station and never be noticed."

Maybe, I thought, but eventually some good person somewhere was bound to find him. What if somebody bad found him?

Dad lowered his head and let out a nervous little cough, as if he'd had the same thought. "Meanwhile," he said, "the police have his description, and the whole force is on the lookout."

It all sounded so drastic to me.

"I know it all sounds pretty drastic," said Dad, "but

we need to cover every possibility. Personally," he smiled at me and tried to look relaxed, "I'm counting on him for supper."

"Me, too," I agreed, too eagerly.

When he didn't show up for dinner, Dad and I sat and pushed the chicken and rice around on our plates in silence. Dad had cooked it special. That's how sure he'd been that Dwayne would be there to eat it. Just like I'd been sure he'd be in the tree house.

During dinner, he called me Nickel three times. It seemed like forever since I'd heard that.

The chicken was dry, though, and the rice gummy. I was starved, so I ate it anyway, trying real hard not to imagine Dwayne sitting cold and hungry in a damp, dangerous storm pipe.

"Dad," I said finally. "Dwayne'll be back before bedtime. His note did say he'd be back, you know. He's not about to sleep outside in the dark somewhere. Besides, it's cold."

"His heavy coat and gloves are gone," said Dad.

"Oh." I jabbed the gummy rice with my fork. But I still thought he'd be back.

"I know he'll be back," said Dad.

Geez, I thought, feeling really close to Dad. He keeps reading my mind.

"But, you know, Nickel, our marriage has been pretty tough on him."

On *him!* I thought.

"Oh?" I said.

"Sure," he answered. "A new house, a new room. He had a much bigger room in his old house. New school district. His mother's last name's not the same as his anymore."

Wow, I thought, their names are different. I'd hate that. I hadn't even thought about that. And a new school. Is that why he doesn't have friends? Did he have friends at his old school?

"One time I saw him staring at the door knocker," said Dad. "It says Kimble. Everybody in this house is a Kimble, everybody but him. And there's the problem with the dog."

"What dog?"

Dad looked surprised. "Dwayne had a Jack Russell terrier. I thought you knew. You should have seen all the tricks he'd taught him. Of course, we couldn't keep him because of my allergies. He gave him up to his cousin in Virginia."

I felt like a fool.

"I had no clue," I mumbled.

"Well," said Dad. "It's been tough on you, too." He reached over and ruffled my hair. "Come on. Let's go watch *Jeopardy* until Dwayne comes home."

Jeopardy, I thought. I'd had one of Dad's home-cooked meals, just him and me, and now we were going to watch *Jeopardy*. Normal life—what I'd wished for. But it didn't feel normal. Not even a little.

Good Knight, Nick 20

Dad and I didn't watch *Jeopardy*. Instead we took turns calling anyone who might know something about Dwayne. Teachers, neighbors, kids in his class. Two hours later, the amount of helpful information we'd rounded up equaled zero.

I tried to focus on my homework, but I kept listening for the phone, the door, anything. Miriam called three times, but there wasn't a trace of Dwayne in Statesville yet. At 10:00 Dad came up to my room.

"Good night, Nick," he said. "Get some sleep. I'll wait up."

"But—"

"No buts. I'll wake you if I hear anything." He picked up Sir Kay. "Is this Dwayne's teddy bear?"

"Dad." I rolled my eyes. "That's Sir Kay."

"Who?" he said.

"Never mind." Good old Dad. Maybe being clueless was hereditary.

I turned off my light and stretched out with my clothes on. No way was I going to sleep. I thought about Dwayne having to give away his dog. No wonder he had practically petted Penelope into a coma.

I thought back to Dwayne's note. "DON'T WORRY. I'LL BE BACK." *When* would he be back? Why would he come back at all if there was nothing here but a door knocker with the wrong name . . . and no dog . . . and me?

Because his mom was here, of course. Besides, where else could he go? His own father hated him.

But what if he did something so awesome his dad wouldn't think he was a wimp anymore? Then he could live with him, maybe even get his dog back, and visit us. Maybe that's what the note meant— he'd be back to visit.

My head hurt from so much thinking, but my insides raced. I felt sure I was onto something.

So, if he could get from here to Statesville by himself, his dad would know he wasn't a baby. Then why wasn't he there by now? It's only sixty miles, and he's been gone all day. A truck would have been there in an hour.

I tried to think of more ways he might prove himself. Ways that would make his dad think he was brave and not a wimp. On Halloween, hadn't Carson called him brave? Brave about what?

Another brick hit me. I knew where Dwayne was. This time I was sure. He was sitting in a field outside of town. In a circle where nothing grew. In Satan's Circle.

I jumped up to go tell Dad. Then I stopped. Dad would go after him and leave me to answer the phone.

I could practically hear my books about knights and warriors whispering to each other from across the room. Would Lancelot send his father to the rescue? Not a chance. Lancelot would do it himself. Even if it was dark. And cold. And dangerous.

My door flew open, and light flooded the room. I squinted at Dad as he stomped over to my bed and shoved the cordless phone in my face.

"It's Magic," he said. "Claims it's urgent. Something about homework. Make it quick." He left the room as suddenly as he'd appeared.

I hadn't even heard the phone ring.

"Hello," I said, trying to sound like I didn't care whether he ever called me again.

"What's up?" said Magic. "Besides you and me, that is." He chuckled, then, before I could open my mouth, he blurted, "Is Dwayne back?"

"No," I answered. Magic's silence on the other end of the receiver made me feel good. He did care. Was that why he'd called?

"Are you calling me about homework?" I asked.

"Heck, no," he said. "I wanted to know about Dwayne." He hesitated. "Uh, Nick. You got any idea where he is?"

"Yes!" I practically screamed into the phone. "I figured it out. Satan's Circle. He's got to be—"

"Yes!" Magic shouted back. "Good thinking!" I heard someone yelling in the background. His parents. Magic lowered his voice. "Has your dad gone to get him?"

"*I'm* going to get him," I answered.

Magic whistled, soft and low. "I'm coming with you," he said, sounding strong and determined.

I heard the crash of a door slamming in his house.

"As soon as my parents go to sleep," he said, his voice trailing off to almost nothing.

"Great," I said, relieved I didn't have to go alone, and glad to have Magic back.

"Nick!" Dad shouted down the hall. "Hang up the phone!"

"Gotta go," I said. "I'll call you when Dad's asleep."

"Okay. Yeah. I'll take the phone to my room."

"Great." I whispered. "We'll shoot for midnight."

Knight or Nut 21

I was pumped. Ready to find Dwayne. Me and Magic. I wanted to go *now*.

Instead, I waited for Dad to fall asleep. And waited. I paced, talked to Sir Kay, checked on Dad. I even cleaned my room. I checked on Dad again and paced some more. The whole time, I pictured Dwayne sitting alone in a dark, scary field.

Finally, around 12:30, Dad started to snore in front of the TV, the cordless phone an inch from his right hand. I sneaked past him toward the kitchen to call Magic on the other phone.

Whack! My foot kicked the coffee table. Dad's snores sputtered twice, then smoothed out again.

I slipped into the kitchen, this time trying to watch Dad *and* where I was going.

I grabbed the phone, wedged myself into the tiny room where our washing machine sits, closed the folding doors, and punched in Magic's number. He answered before the first ring even finished.

"You ready?" I asked.

I heard loud voices in the background.

"I can't," said Magic. "Not yet. My parents. Can you give me more time?"

"How much?"

"I don't know," he said.

"Magic." I hesitated. My heart was about to leap out of my chest I was so ready to go. "I could wait a little while, but—"

"I know," he said. "You'd better go. There's no telling when . . . " His voice trailed off.

"Magic," I said, "thanks for trying."

"Sure," he said. "Be careful."

I clicked off the receiver, made sure Dad was still asleep, and slipped out the back door. Nick. To the rescue.

I grabbed my bike, feeling like a real hero, and took off so fast down the driveway that, turning into the street, I almost spun out. I'd pedaled four blocks before it hit me. I was going alone. No Magic.

I noticed how strange our neighborhood felt. Eerie vibrations in the air, like a ghost town, with one lone ghost dog howling somewhere behind me. Was I crazy? I bet even Lancelot didn't go around rescuing people after midnight.

No. I clenched my teeth and gripped the handlebars tighter. I needed to stop thinking about knights and start acting like one.

By the time I got to the edge of town and headed into the country, the dark empty night seemed even creepier. I felt less like a knight by the minute—and more like a nut. What was I doing riding my bike down a deserted, dusty road at one o'clock in the morning?

Why hadn't I waited for Magic? What if Dad woke up? What if Dwayne had come home?

My eyes adjusted to the dark, but I couldn't always see what was in the road. Twice I hit rocks and nearly pitched off my bike. My fingers started to ache from the cold and from gripping the handlebars so tightly. Why hadn't I worn gloves?

I formed a new list in my mind.

1. Think before you act.

2. If you decide to act, think again.

Once, I saw headlights and panicked. Where could I hide? But the clowns in the Mustang that roared by wouldn't have noticed me if I'd been wearing Day-Glo. They were too busy throwing beer cans at mailboxes.

Then back to silence so loud I could hear it. Not even a cricket. Just inky black darkness, and that hollow feeling in the air—the one that makes you feel alone, but watched.

As I got closer to the old farm where Satan's Circle was, I entered a stretch of woods. Tree limbs, blacker than the sky, hunkered over me like huge spiders. Why had all those rescues in *King Arthur* seemed so exciting? Maybe if I were riding a mighty steed instead of a wobbly bike, or wearing a coat of armor instead of a ratty fleece jacket. Yeah, that might help.

What would it mean if I found Satan's Circle empty? That Dwayne had been body-snatched into a void like Derek's grandmother's cow? Or that he was snug in Statesville with Miriam, drinking hot chocolate and getting hugged?

Finally. I spotted the split rail fence that marked the property Satan's Circle sat on. The rails looked like a pile of bleached bones stacked in the darkness.

I leaned my bike against them, blew some warmth back into my hands, and climbed over.

"Dwayne?" I whispered.

Nothing.

I clicked on my flashlight and swept the field with light. Tall dead grass, a huge tree to my left, some bushes. No Dwayne.

I took a deep breath and crept forward, my feet making enough crunching noises on the dried grass stalks to wake Dracula. The flashlight beam made me feel even more exposed, like a voice shouting, "Here I am!"

I clicked it off.

Deep, soundless, sinister darkness.

Except for my heart.

I stopped to let my eyes adjust again, and to remind myself to breathe.

That's when I spotted it, off to the right, the place where there was no tall grass—because nothing grew there. A big circular clearing with a dark lump in it.

"Dwayne?' I called softly.

The dark lump shifted.

My heart leaped right out of my chest. I clicked my flashlight back on and aimed it at the blob. It was

Dwayne. Looking small. But not scared. No. He sat cross-legged and wise, like Yoda from *The Empire Strikes Back*, gazing confidently into my beam of light.

"Hi, Nick," he said proudly. His voice didn't squeak at all.

Objects Don't Vanish 22

Hi, Nick? Was that the best Dwayne could come up with? He sat in the dark on a cursed patch of mystery dirt at one-thirty in the morning, and all he could say was "Hi, Nick"?

"Are you crazy?" I shouted at him, still shining my flashlight in his face. I marched over to the edge of the circle, but I didn't step in it. "Do you know how worried your mother is?"

"I'm sorry," said Dwayne matter-of-factly, as though it couldn't be helped.

"Come on, then. Let's go home."

"No," he answered stubbornly.

"Look," I said, impatient to be out of there. "I'm sorry I said all those things about your mother."

Dwayne sagged. For a long time, he didn't say anything. A train whistle blew in the distance.

"Mom didn't go to your coach," he answered, hanging his head. "I did."

I clicked off my flashlight.

"I know," I said sympathetically. "But it's okay. You were just trying to help." I motioned him to come on. I hoped he hadn't noticed that while he sat squarely in Satan's Circle, I hung on the outside—a good fifteen feet away.

"Dwayne," I said, "it doesn't matter. Let's just go home." I turned to leave.

"I can't," Dwayne answered.

I turned back, edging as close to the bare dirt boundary as I could get without actually touching it. "Don't make me drag you out of there."

"I'm staying all night," returned Dwayne.

"Well, I'm not." I stomped off. Halfway back to my bike, my guilty conscience nagged. *You can't leave him.*

This rescue was not going according to plan.

I trudged back, stopping at the edge of the circle where nothing grew. "It's only a stupid superstition," I muttered to myself.

I held my breath and stepped onto the bare dirt. I didn't disappear, but I swear my foot tingled. And the air was noticeably colder.

I eased down on the ground beside Dwayne.

"Look," I said, trying to sound nice, "I know about your dad and you. But there's a million other ways you can prove to him that you're not a wimp. I'll help you. Okay?"

Dwayne was quiet for what seemed like forever.

Finally he said, "I'm not doing this to prove something to my dad." He hesitated. "I'm doing it to prove something to you."

We sat for a long time after that, neither of us saying a word. "Dwayne," I said at last, "you are definitely not a wimp."

"Really?" he asked cautiously. "How about a dork? Am I still a dork?"

I hesitated a second too long. "No. Of course not."

"I'm still a dork," he said flatly.

"Uh, sometimes your mom buys you cool clothes," I explained, "but you wear them funny."

"Funny?" he repeated. "What do you mean, *funny?*"

"Well," I said, "look at your shoes."

We both looked at his shoes. They were so white they glowed in the dark.

"They look fine to me," he said.

I clicked on my flashlight and aimed the light at his clean, neatly laced sneakers. Then I shined it on my dirty, scuffed, half-laced ones.

"Oh," he said. "I thought you couldn't afford new ones."

"These *are* new," I said.

Dwayne half-choked, then thought a minute. "No kidding," he answered quietly. I could practically hear his brain working on a revised shoe theory.

He stood up and slowly began to rub the toes of his shoes in the dirt.

"And pull your shirttail out," I directed.

He tugged on his shirt.

"Get it dirty," I said, right before I tackled him. I wrenched off one shoe, grabbed a rock, and scraped the leather.

Dwayne giggled, jerked off his other shoe, and ground it into the dirt. We threw both of them to the ground and jumped up and down on them, laughing like maniacs.

I dropped a fistful of dirt on his head. "And do something about your hair!" I shouted.

Dwayne sat up, shook the dust out of his hair, and combed it back into place with his fingers.

"I like my hair," he said.

I stared at him. Even in the dark, the perfect hair *was* Dwayne.

"Fair enough," I agreed.

I stretched out on the ground, with my hands behind my head, and looked up at the black sky. Dwayne sat cross-legged. About a million stars twinkled at me.

Me and Dwayne, I chuckled to myself, *in Satan's Circle*. Wait till Carson hears about this.

Carson. I wondered if he'd gotten caught for lying. Or for smoking. Probably not. Did I even care? Yeah, actually I did.

"How'd you find this place?" I asked.

"I called Magic for directions," he answered, "but I made him swear not to tell."

"You're kidding." I sat bolt upright. Then I lay back flat. That explained a lot.

"Did he?" asked Dwayne.

"Did he what?"

"Tell?"

"Nope." I smiled. "But he called to make sure I figured it out."

"Oh," said Dwayne. He sounded like that was a good thing. "Can I see your flashlight?" he asked. "I want to look at my new shoes."

"Sure." I reached for it in the dark. Where was it?

I swept my hand over the bare ground. No flashlight.

"We must have knocked it away," I said, getting up to look.

Dwayne looked, too. No flashlight. A blast of icy air swirled across my face and vanished into the night as quickly as it had come. My feet tingled again.

"Nick," said Dwayne, "you don't think—"

"Nah," I assured him. "It's just a superstition. Objects don't vanish." But I didn't feel sure. "Time to go home anyway, don't you think?"

"Not yet," said Dwayne.

I tried to relax, gazing at the stars and thinking how I'd never be one. Mostly I wondered where in the heck the flashlight was.

"I know how you can be a starter," Dwayne said out of nowhere.

"Yeah?" I humored him.

"Yeah. Work on your three-point shot and you'll be better than Paul at number two guard."

And not play point guard, I thought. It did make more sense than competing with Carson. Too bad I'd probably be kicked off the team for missing today's game. But all I said was "Good plan, Dwayne. Thanks."

"You're welcome."

The hoot of an owl made the hair on the back of my neck goose-bump up.

Another wind gust rattled the leaves of a tree off to my right. I scanned the bare ground, still hoping to see my flashlight.

I was way past ready to be back in my room, in my bed, but I wasn't about to beg. "Hey," I said, remembering Dwayne's room, "can you teach me how to play chess?"

"Yes," he answered. "Definitely."

Dwayne still sat calm and cross-legged. I thought about Yoda, and *Star Wars* and Jedi knights, knights of the future, with light sabers and land cruisers instead of swords and horses.

"Dwayne," I said, "in the dark you look like Yoda."

He giggled and lowered his voice. "Go, you must," he mimicked.

"Not without you," I answered.

I felt his smile light up the night.

"Let's go home," he said.

We raced for my bike. I don't know about Dwayne, but I was majorly happy that all Satan had snagged was a flashlight.

New Stuff I Learned 23

1. Dwayne is braver than me.
2. Chigger bites itch for eight days.
3. Sneaking out at night will get me grounded, even if I have a good reason.
4. Coach thinks looking for a missing brother *is* an excused absence.
5. Don't ever make promises to people after they die.
6. Dwayne gets motion sick riding on the back of my bike.
7. It's hard to be a good brother to someone who has thrown up on you twice.

It's been three weeks since Dwayne and I stumbled home from Satan's Circle, but it seems like a year ago. Dad zoomed through about a trillion emotions in less than a minute. First, he was relieved.

Then joyful, hugging us so hard I'm surprised we didn't snap. Next, he called Miriam. Then, he got mad. Three seconds later, he went ballistic.

At school the next day, I was a hero. Not because I'd saved Dwayne, but because I'd gotten grounded. For sneaking out. And for sitting in Satan's Circle at one in the morning. I can't decide if that means doing stupid stuff makes you popular, or brave stuff does. When I figure it out, I'll add it to my list.

Carson did not get busted, but Miriam swears that one day it will all catch up with him. Meanwhile, she's treating me like Lancelot for saving Dwayne. Has she forgotten that I'm the one who made him run away?

Dwayne. He reads, draws, cooks, and waters his man-eating plants. I shoot baskets. Once in a while, we play chess. Sometimes he drives me crazy, but not like before. Life with him is a lot like Miriam's food. Some days I get pizza, other days—tofu.

Magic and I are back to normal. He didn't have a clue how to handle Dwayne's secret. He wanted to tell me, but he kept seeing Dwayne, round-eyed and trusting, counting on him not to.

Meanwhile, I'm working like a maniac on my three-point shot. As soon as I can hit ten in a row without missing, I'm going to surprise Coach. Yesterday, I got to nine. *Swish, swish, swish.* Nothing but net. I was on a roll. The next two didn't swish—they hit the backboard and went in. That counts. Then, four more swishes.

I'm that close.

Acknowledgments

My deepest thanks go to
Lisa Thalhimer, Joan Carris, Judy Crowder,
Nancy Tilly, and Dee Hamilton, for all their
many helpful thoughts and suggestions,
and for keeping me writing.